THE SPIDER:
THE CITY OF LOST MEN

MASTER OF MEN!

THE SPIDER

THE CITY
OF LOST MEN

By Grant Stockbridge

STEEGER BOOKS • 2021

CHAPTER 1
MANY GO MAD

NOTHING COULD have been more peaceful than the smoothly flowing traffic along Central Park West; nor could anything have been less exciting than the social call Richard Wentworth had in prospect. Yet, his senses were sharply attuned to an indefinable premonition of danger as he sat at the wheel of his sedan, covertly studying the lovely face of the girl beside him. Nita van Sloan was troubled, and her uneasiness reached out invisible fingers that told him the truth—despite her attempts to conceal her agitation.

"This was going to be a quiet evening in front of your hearth," he commented. "Seems to me, I recall hearing your vow that a team of horses could not drag you out—"

"I know, Dick," she interrupted nervously. "I *did* want to stay home… but I couldn't refuse Alicia. She seemed so anxious to have us come tonight. Her voice was tense, so excited—it made me feel that she was afraid of something. When I hesitated, she fairly *begged* me! I wish she hadn't called—and yet, somehow, I wish we were with her right now."

So did Wentworth—but he did not say so.

In all probability, he told himself, Alicia Sprague was troubled by nothing more than some domestic problem she desired to talk over with Nita. They would go off into a huddle for most of the evening, and he would be left with Dr. Thornton Sprague,

The armory was being looted of guns and ammunition!

her father. Though he might be one of the most efficient presidents Columbia University had ever had, the old gentleman was far from being an absorbing after-dinner companion. Undoubtedly, that was the way it would work out… and yet Wentworth pushed his foot down harder on the accelerator.…

"It isn't like her to become upset," Nita worried. "I can't imagine what is on her mind. Why was she so anxious for me to bring you with me, unless—"

Whatever Nita had been about to say was forgotten, gulped back in a startled gasp as she stiffened, feet braced against the floor-boards, her partly outstretched hand fighting back the

temptation to grasp Wentworth's arm at the wheel. Simultaneously, Wentworth's gaze flashed from the delicate oval of her face to the light-splotched asphalt which stretched away in front of them.

Siren wailing eerily, a police car had whizzed past the sedan and was now streaking down the avenue, crazily. From side to side, as if a drunken man were driving, it careened ahead—then went wild altogether. Shooting off at a tangent, it suddenly cut across the roadway, climbed up onto the sidewalk, and crashed full-tilt into a lamp-post.

Nita snapped the back of a hand against her lips to check a half-scream, as the patrol car bounced off the post and turned over. Wentworth's deep-set, blue-gray eyes were gleaming out of his tense face. He swung toward the curb. Before he could reach it, another police car came racing madly out of a side street.

Wailing like a lost soul, this second car sped in a wild arc across the avenue, apparently completely out of control. For an instant, Wentworth was certain that a head-on collision was inevitable, as the mad machine swerved and came squarely at him. He stepped on the gas and spurted ahead, clearing disaster by inches. Then came the crash of the smash-up, the groan of rending metal.

The next car in the line behind him was the victim. The second police coupé had caught it broadside, telescoped against it—and then, as an explosion seemed to tear away the entire hood and windshield frame, burst into flames. Like a rag-doll, a blue-uniformed figure catapulted out of the wreckage and skidded across the pavement.

THAT MUCH Wentworth had glimpsed in his rear-view mirror, as he jammed on the brakes. Now he was out of the door, running to the fallen man. By some miracle, the sergeant had not been seriously injured. Groggily, he got to his feet, shaking his head as if to clear it. Wentworth concluded that the shock had momentarily stunned him... until he glimpsed the wild look in the man's eyes.

Instantly, that look flashed a message to Wentworth's brain. A definite sense of calamity gripped him, as he observed the vacuous grin on the officer's face, heard the chuckling mumble that came from loose lips. Quickly, Wentworth turned, raced back to his own car and switched on the radio. With it tuned to the police frequency, he manipulated the finding knob, until the police announcer's voice came in.

"Calling Cars Seventy-two and Ninety-six," the monotone was directing. "Proceed immediately to Six-fifty Central Park West, the home of Doctor Thornton Sprague. Emergency call."

The home of Dr. Thornton Sprague—their own destination! Wentworth's nerves tingled. But his poker face was expressionless, as he slipped behind the wheel, threw the car into gear. His sixth sense had not failed him; more than mere feminine caprice had been behind Alicia Sprague's urgent invitation.

Nita's violet eyes were round with alarm, yet she remained silent. Too experienced at this sort of thing, accustomed to coming face to face with peril, she knew better than to give way to emotions. A warm glow surged through Richard Wentworth, as he darted an appreciative glance at her set expression. A woman in a million was Nita van Sloan. The only woman in the world—if only he could take her. If only he could give her the love and protection, the peace and happiness, she so richly deserved....

Like icy fingers, closing around his heart, came the realization that he could not do these things. He could offer little but the prospect of trouble and uncertainty, ceaseless worry and mental torture—so long as he felt it his duty to take up the gauntlet for the helpless and downtrodden, at the mercy of the human leeches who fatten on their fellows' misery.

So long as cunning criminals, safe in their immunity to the law, could operate successfully, he knew that there would be no peace for him. So long as brazen underworld chieftains could laugh at the futile efforts of the police, he knew that he could not lie back in the comfort his wealth could command. So long as human rights and liberties tottered in precarious jeopardy, beneath the onslaughts of society's ruthless enemies, there would be a need for the strange creature of the night men called the Spider. The Spider must don his ebon habiliments and take the vengeance trail through the tortuous byways of crime. No comforts of home, no soft arms of a loving wife, could there be for Richard Wentworth!

Before the pang of these thoughts had ceased to stab through his heart, his agile mind was focusing upon this latest problem, groping for the tie that must exist between those crazily gyrating police cars and his own visit to the home of Columbia University's president.

And then the Sprague home loomed up ahead.

A LARGE sedan was starting away from in front of the building. Another stood at the curb, its door open as dark figures crowded through it—men who were moving with frantic haste.

Before these men could jam their way into the car, Wentworth's sedan had squealed to a skidding stop behind it.

"Down, Nita—behind the dashboard!" he barked as he swung through the door. He flattened himself on the street as a fusillade of bullets abruptly whined over his head.

Flat on his stomach, he inched his way to the scant protection of the curbstone while his own guns blazed at the fleeing gunmen. Two dived head-foremost into the tonneau of the car, and the machine started to get under way. Before it was clear of the curb, Wentworth's sedan swept out in front, partially blocked it.

Crouched low over the wheel, Nita tried desperately to trap them—to smash them up, if necessary. She almost succeeded. Then the thugs' car climbed over the curb, cut so deeply onto the sidewalk that it almost grazed the house-fronts. It circled back into the roadway, as its door slammed shut.

Those few seconds of delay cost the life of one of their number. Clinging to the side of the car, trying frantically to hurl himself through the doorway, the fellow had been fully exposed to Wentworth's fire. It was for but a fraction of a second—yet two bullets found lodging in his brain and his heart.

With a final burst of spiteful fire, far wide of its mark, the fleeing machine sped down the street. Wentworth scrambled erect. His flat-planed, vital face filled with concern as he darted a glance at his car. But Nita had already stopped it and was running toward him, as he started for the doorway of the Sprague home.

That doorway, he saw at once, stood open—and he understood why. It was propped wide by the dead body of Martin, the Sprague butler who sprawled in the pool of blood that seeped from his battered skull.

Nita caught her breath, and clutched at Wentworth's arm. Then she followed him around the body and was running anxiously through the hall, calling the name of her friend.

"Alicia! Alicia!" The walls threw back the echo emptily. It was the only sound in the building—until Wentworth caught a weak half-moan that seemed to come from the living-room. Then he stopped.

They had rushed through that room and, in their quick search for Alicia, had seen nobody. But now, when Wentworth retraced his footsteps, he located the feeble sound. It came from behind a large desk, where Dr. Sprague lay on the floor, trying hopelessly to get to his hands and knees. Blood was pouring down from his head, drenching his face, and Wentworth saw that another crimson fount was spouting from his chest, matting on the white shirt-front.

Instantly Wentworth was at the stricken man's side, raising his head and trying to wipe the blood from his face. Sprague tried to speak, but his voice was no more than a husky, gurgling whisper.

"Alicia," Wentworth made out the girl's name. Then there was something that sounded like, "Madman… gone… loose madman—Scott… taken Alicia—"

The old man managed to raise his right hand and the clutching fingers loosened—to reveal a peculiar, putty-like figure clamped tight in his palm. Glassy-eyed, he stared at the thing. A spasm passed through him, that contorted his face with horror, left his body limp, lifeless.

Gently, Wentworth pried the dead fingers wide and took from their grasp an oval object about two and a half inches long, a relief of a human face cast in what appeared to be soap—a face that leered up at him with the horrible, idiot stare of a madman! HE WAS still kneeling beside the body, gazing, nonplussed, at that devilishly realistic cast, when he suddenly became aware that others were arriving. Footsteps and men's voices sounded outside in the hallway. Standing in the doorway was a large, florid-faced man who regarded Wentworth with narrowed eyes before he stepped into the room.

Victor Hanson, publisher of the *Evening Standard*, walked forward as if he were treading on eggs. His large, protuberant eyes fairly popped out as he gaped at the blood-drenched face of the corpse.

"You're on hand mighty soon—even for a newspaperman, Hanson," Wentworth flung at him before the other could force intelligible words through twitching lips. "What are you doing here?"

"He—Doctor Sprague—telephoned and asked me to come,"

the publisher stammered. "He sounded excited about something—so I hurried over. Now he's dead—"

"How long ago was that?" Wentworth pressed.

"Twenty—it couldn't have been more than half an hour," Hanson answered meekly, his usual pomposity absent as he reacted to the unmistakable note of authority in Wentworth's whip-lashing voice.

Alicia had been frantic in her appeal to Nita to come there and bring Wentworth with her; Dr. Sprague had been excited when he urged Hanson to call—if the publisher could be believed. Now Alicia had vanished and her father was dead—murdered and left clutching an idiot talisman in his stiffening fingers....

Wentworth remembered those smashed police cars, the wild look in the dazed sergeant's eyes. But before he could follow his thoughts farther, the police were on hand—surging into the room, pumping questions at him. Nita's corroboration, and the dead body of the thug outside on the sidewalk, quickly established Wentworth's story. Then two officers came in. With them was a special patrolman, who had been on guard outside the Sprague home, and the regular policeman on the beat.

"I found this feller walking alone, across the street by the park," reported the man who had brought in the watchman. "He was laughing to himself, and going on the way he's doing now."

"Same with this one." The bluecoat, who had located his fellow officer, turned awe-stricken eyes on the man he had rounded up. "He was sitting down the block on the curb, talkin' to himself."

Both the stricken men were vacant-eyed, mumbling meaningless words to themselves, chuckling soundlessly. They seemed to have no conception of what was going on around them or of their surroundings—until someone approached and tried to touch them. The wrists of each, Wentworth noticed, were red and swollen. When he took the watchman's arm, and tried to raise it for closer inspection, the man backed away from him, fearfully.

"No more... no more... no more..." came endlessly from the slack lips, and haunting terror was in the staring eyes.

Aside from swollen wrists, the victims seemed unmarked—stricken with madness as if an evil wand had been merely waved over their heads. Nothing about them gave any clue to what had happened—until their pockets were searched.

Out of the watchman's coat pocket came one of those mad soap faces, and the policeman's trousers pocket yielded one identical. Two idiotic masks, counterparts of the one Thornton Sprague's dying fingers had clutched!

Wentworth cast a glance at the wide-eyed police. More than one face was blanched. Terror—grisly fear of the unknown—was gripping these men who would have thought nothing of facing blazing guns or the cold steel of a knife edge. Uneasily, they exchanged glances, then stared at those mumbling madmen.

IT WAS at that moment that Police Commissioner Stanley Kirkpatrick arrived. A sergeant strode in to make way for him. For a moment, the commissioner stood framed in the doorway—a handsome, florid-faced man in his late forties, with the air of dignity and authority that comes with years of command. His saturnine face was expressionless, as he stared at the corpse.

Yet, the moment he spied those brainless mumblers, Wentworth was certain that a bit of the healthy color left his cheeks. Kirkpatrick's eyes narrowed, almost as if flinching.

He nodded curtly to Wentworth and Nita, and listened, while the sergeant who had taken charge in the death-room explained what had occurred.

"Who is this man who was killed outside?" he cut in as soon as the sergeant finished his account. "Have you identified him?"

"He's Goober Nelson, Commissioner," a detective volunteered. "Ran with Manny Green's mob. Torpedo with half a dozen notches on his gun but slick enough to wiggle out every time—until now."

"There is always a rap they can't beat," Kirkpatrick said with unmistakable satisfaction, and the glance he flashed at Wentworth was warm with commendation.

Manny Green, Wentworth knew, had consumed a considerable portion of Kirkpatrick's time during the past few months. Working hand in hand with Barry Winant, a special prosecutor appointed by the governor, the commissioner had waged relentless war against the city-wide policy racket—a campaign that had reached its culmination with the conviction of Manny Green, the acknowledged policy king. Only that afternoon, Green had been taken off to Sing Sing to begin serving sentence.

The gunman who had died on the sidewalk had been one of Manny's henchmen. Apparently he and the others who had escaped in the cars were in some way connected with this curious madness and the maniacal faces that seemed to symbolize it. What that connection was, Wentworth could not imagine.

During the past week there had been two robberies reported, and noteworthy because the patrolman on duty in each case had been found stricken with madness. Recollection of those cases had flashed into Wentworth's mind when he saw the dazed, wild-eyed expression of the sergeant from the smashed patrol car. The cancer that was eating its way into the police department had gone far deeper than he knew.

Kirkpatrick drew him and Nita aside into one of the other rooms, while waiting for the medical examiner to arrive. The commissioner's face was lined with worry. He brushed his spiked mustache with the first knuckle of his right hand—which told Wentworth more emphatically than any words that he was deeply agitated.

"So far I have managed to keep the magnitude of the thing from the press—managed to suppress the details in most of the cases—but this, tonight, will break all over the front pages," the commissioner said. "This isn't only the third case, as you probably suppose. There have been more than a dozen, scattered through all parts of the city—and, in each case, the victim has been rendered incurably insane." He took a deep breath.

"I've managed to keep most of this out of the papers. Yet, despite my efforts to hush it up, the news of this strange mental blight has sped along the department grapevine. It's spreading like wildfire. A thing like this can be appallingly dangerous, if it isn't nipped in the bud. It can demoralize the entire force, if it gets out of hand. I don't know how to fight it—or I didn't until you put those bullets into Goober Nelson."

"You think Manny Green's gang is behind it?" Wentworth

asked, face filled with concern, as he watched the commissioner's lips working worriedly.

They were a striking pair, those two—Kirkpatrick, upstanding and erect, his face lined with unmistakable character, hair tinged with the gray that comes with long years of crime-fighting; Wentworth, tall, perfectly poised, square-shouldered, strong-featured face topped with a head of crisp black hair.

Between them existed a friendship based on mutual respect and admiration. More than once, Richard Wentworth had risked his life in order to snatch the commissioner from death. Kirkpatrick would, just as quickly, have faced extinction to keep from harm this amateur criminologist who often had proved more invaluable to him than his entire department. Yet, friends though they were, between them stood a wraith, a specter—the wavering, uncertain figure of the Spider.

Kirkpatrick, a man of the law, could not abide private vengeance, no matter how great its provocation. Even though the resources of his department were exhausted, and a fiendish criminal might be laughing at him, he would not countenance the Spider's taking the law into his own hands. While he fully realized and appreciated the salutary effect of this grim nemesis upon the cowering minions of the underworld, Stanley Kirkpatrick was sworn to capture the Spider and bring him to justice as he would any other who stepped outside the law.

Was Wentworth really the Spider? Kirkpatrick was morally certain of it—yet could not prove it. Had definite proof come into his hands, Wentworth would not be standing there beside him now, a free man....

"I have nothing definite on which to pin my suspicions, Dick," Kirkpatrick answered the question, after a thoughtful pause. "But the day Manny Green was convicted, you remember, he bitterly declared that he had been framed, and warned me and Barry Winant that we could not close his case merely by bundling him off to prison. That very night a policeman was found grinning foolishly as he patrolled in front of a large jewelry store that had been looted." He frowned.

"He was the first of the madness victims. Since then, the thing has been happening with the frightfulness of an epidemic. From all parts of the city, I have had reports of robberies perpetrated under the noses of the police—squarely in sight of officers who stand by and raise no finger to interfere because they have been stricken hopelessly insane. How the thing strikes we have no idea. The best doctors have not been able to diagnose it, which makes it more terrifying. Like a poisonous virus, the fear it generates is working its way throughout the force. Yet, at last we've got something on which to work. Now that we've identified Goober Nelson—!"

The wail of oncoming police sirens chopped off his words, and Kirkpatrick stood as if he waited for another blow to strike. Wentworth ran across the room to a window and yanked the control ropes of the Venetian blinds that screened it.

Down the avenue came two patrol cars, sirens wide open, streaking along as if coming down the last stretch in a race. Past the house they sped, and then swung around on squealing tires to disappear into one of the transverse roads that cut across Central Park.

CHAPTER 2
DEATH IN THE NIGHT

THE SCREAMING sirens, which momentarily had paralyzed Kirkpatrick, now shocked him out of his stupefaction. He galvanized into action. Dashing into the hallway, he ran to a telephone, barking a demand for headquarters. But Wentworth did not wait to learn the result of that call.

Nor did Nita. She needed no direction. So perfectly was her mind coördinated with Wentworth's, she fairly read his thoughts. Before he whirled from the window, she was already at the door, tugging it open, to race across the sidewalk and to the waiting sedan. She was at the wheel, when Wentworth leaped in beside her—and then they were off in pursuit of the vanished patrol cars.

As they swung into the transverse road, Wentworth's eyes peered ahead, straining for a glimpse of the fading police tail-lights. His mind was busily at work, analyzing what had happened.

Thornton Sprague must have feared trouble, and so must Alicia. But why? What connection could the sedate university president and his daughter possibly have had with denizens of the underworld? How could they have become tied up with this mysterious blight of madness that Kirkpatrick feared would demoralize his entire force?

Barry Winant, Wentworth recalled, had been a member of the Columbia faculty—dean of the law school. He had resigned to accept the governor's appointment as special prosecutor.

Could that be the connection, between Sprague, Winant and Manny Green, that had brought death to Sprague and resulted in his daughter's disappearance?

Alicia—what had happened to her? Had she been kidnaped, dragged off in one of those fleeing cars? Or had she vanished even before the thugs invaded her home?

Victor Hanson—where did he fit into the picture? Was it fear for his own safety that had impelled Sprague to summon the publisher—or was it concern for Alicia? Hanson, Wentworth knew, had long been one of Alicia's suitors; now he seemed greatly concerned about her disappearance. Wentworth did not like the man, despised the yellow journalism that was all that kept the *Evening Standard* alive. But, still, he strove to be fair....

Nita stepped on the gas until the accelerator was almost flush with the floorboards. The specially built motor, beneath the custom hood, was humming like a great dynamo; the car was fairly rocketing through the little-traveled crossroad.

"There they are—just ahead," she exclaimed excitedly, "turning into Fifth Avenue." Then she was braking, to careen into the avenue with scarcely slackened speed.

A few blocks down the avenue, the police cars whipped in to the curb. Now Wentworth saw a dozen others already lined up there, bluecoats piling out of them and rushing into the park.

Before Nita had the car fully stopped, he leaped from the running-board and sprinted across the sidewalk to where several policemen held back the gathering crowd from something that sprawled on the park walk close to the entrance. With a shudder of horror, he saw the body of a young woman, so viciously knifed and mangled that it was covered with blood from head to foot!

Beside it on the walk sat a dazed young man, bleeding head between his hands. He stared incredulously at the ghastly sight which the police were now covering with a sheet.

"Laura—Laura honey," he moaned, swaying drunkenly. "I tried to save you, honey—tried to fight them off. They were too many for me. There must have been hundreds—thousands of them—the murdering rats!"

Tears were streaming down his cheeks. Wentworth saw that he was half-delirious, still stunned by the blows that must have knocked him out. Nor was he the only one. Several of the policemen were returning, bringing other young fellows, clothing torn, faces bruised and battered. The victims seemed too dazed to know what had happened; some fought hysterically to be allowed to plunge back into the darkness of the park.

"She's in there—Edna's in there!" one of them screamed, as he struggled to tear loose from the arms of a burly bluecoat. "Those rotten devils have her! You're not going to make me leave her there! I'm going after her—"

It took two officers to hold him back, and, when Wentworth caught a glimpse of his eyes, he saw horror had driven the lad half-mad.

There were eight of these young fellows, and their stories were identical. They had come with their girls, to spend the evening in the park. They had been sitting on benches, or walking along the paths—without a suspicion of danger—when suddenly men had leaped out from the bushes, surrounding them. Before they

18

knew what had happened, they had been borne to the ground. Their girls were seized, dragged off into the bushes.

"Betty broke away from them," one boy gasped out his nightmare experience. "She tried to run back to me—but one of those devils caught her by her dress and ripped it off. She was screaming, but they laughed at her and picked her up. Then I didn't hear anything, and she was gone!"

The path was now swarming with policemen, and a captain had arrived to take charge. Quickly, he organized and detailed his men, blocking off all approaches to that section of the park, surrounding the area in which the attacks had occurred.

"We comb every square foot of this place," he growled. "I want you men to stay so close to one another that not even a squirrel will be able to slip through the cordon. I want those girls—and the rats who grabbed them!"

NITA, WENTWORTH saw, was standing uncertainly beside the sedan. Running back to the machine, he cautioned her not to leave it. Then, before she could protest, he was back in the park, identifying himself to the police captain as a friend of Kirkpatrick's and following on the heels of the officers who were already beginning to spread the dragnet that should round up the attackers.

Slowly, the cordon moved forward, flashlights playing into every dark spot, nightsticks prodding every clump of bushes, swinging down at every suspicious-looking shadow. All along the line, Wentworth could hear the sound of their progress, catch low-spoken words as the grim-faced hunters kept in contact with one another.

Close at their heels he followed, alert to catch the slightest indication that any of the quarry might have slipped through the closing dragnet. There seemed to be nobody but the police in the surrounded area—not a living soul—until suddenly he stared into the round-eyed, frightened face of a girl crouching low in a clump of shrubbery!

Suddenly men had leaped
wildly at them from the
surrounding bushes!

That face—he knew it well! But, as their eyes met, he saw that
she had no suspicion of his identity.

In the same split-second, a young fellow suddenly popped to
his feet beside the girl—a young fellow who swung a blackjack at

21

the head of the policeman just in front of Wentworth. Without a sound, the cop crumpled and dropped to the ground—but not before one of his mates leaped forward, gun leveled at the young fellows head. A finger tightened on the trigger.

Wentworth heard the girl's half-stifled cry of terror, saw her spring to her feet and try to throw herself in the way of the bullet—and in that moment he acted. Leaping between them, he brought his right fist rocketing upward in a merciful upper-cut. It landed on the point of the cop's jaw, lifted him from his feet. Diving beneath him, Wentworth caught the body before it could crash to the ground and attract further attention.

That was all the opportunity the girl and her companion needed. Taking advantage of their chance to break through the police line, they rushed past Wentworth. Half-minded to pursue and bring them back, he turned and saw them racing across a lawn. At the same time, he beheld Nita in the distance. She had followed him into the park and must have seen what he had just done now....

Before he had time to make a move, another bluecoat blundered into him; caught him sidewise and almost knocked him off balance. Wentworth threw his arms out and caught at the cop to keep from falling, whirled him around—and saw that the man's eyes were blank, the face twisted in a silly grin. Instead of helping in the search, he was wandering aimlessly through the park, mumbling and chuckling insanely.

A few minutes ago, those officers had been in perfect control of their senses—and now this one had become a brainless idiot! Did that mean that this blight of madness was at work here in the park—might strike out of the darkness and snatch its unsuspecting victims from the very midst of their fellows?

Wentworth could feel a chill coursing up his spine, goose-pimpling his skin as he peered into the dark shadows all around him.

"What happened to you?" he demanded as he shook the officer and tried to bring him back to his senses. "Snap out of it, man! You've *got* to help us fight this thing!"

But when he took his man to a lamp-post, and stared into the vacuous eyes, he knew effort was useless. The bluecoat could only grin, had not even sufficient muscular control to keep the saliva from drooling down his sagging chin. By his collar markings, Wentworth saw that he was attached to the twenty-second precinct.

The twenty-second was the Central Park precinct, stationed in the old arsenal. The building should be only a short distance away. Wentworth began leading his unresisting companion toward it, his racing brain endeavoring to solve this deviltry.

Before he arrived at the arsenal, he saw that he was not alone in his course. Blue-coated figures were converging on it from several directions—always two, and sometimes three, together—one or two leading another. Like him, they were bringing in their stricken mates!

When he reached the station, the awe-stricken patrolmen had gathered together half a dozen of their fellows—all idiot victims who wandered about aimlessly and chatted meaningless nothings to themselves. Six strong men, who had suddenly been plunged into a mental darkness that made them more helpless

than children! Lost souls doomed to a living death behind the bars of some lonely sanitarium!
SILENTLY, THEY were shepherded inside, their mates hardly daring to touch them—as if each feared that even such slight contact might spread the fearful contamination. They were brought inside and lined up in front of a desk—from which a gray-haired sergeant looked down with rheumy, uncomprehending eyes!

Now some of the reserve officers were coming out of their quarters, gathering around the stricken men, amazed and horrified by the transformation that had come over them.

"God A'mighty!" one of them exclaimed, as he tried to talk to one of the victims, but was rewarded by nothing but a zany grin. "He was all right when he relieved me an hour ago. *Now* look at him!"

In uncomprehending terror, the others drew back from those poor creatures who, in less than sixty minutes, had been transformed into lost souls wandering blindly through the fog of endless mental night. Incredulously, they stared up at the desk sergeant, now gaping vacantly at something that lay on the blotter in front of him.

Wentworth did not have to step up behind the desk to see the thing which fascinated the old man. It was the soap mask of a face that leered up at him with an expression even more maniacal than his own!

24

Not only could this baffling curse snatch at its victims, as they paced their beats; it could reach right into the precinct station, cast its damning spell upon the man on duty....

Kirkpatrick had arrived and was in charge, when Wentworth went back to the entrance of the park. The avenue, he saw at once, was jammed with curiosity-seekers. They were being held back by reserves, summoned from surrounding precincts. Now another body was stretched out beside the corpse of the mangled girl.

"This young feller tried to fight for his girl," one of the blue-coats told Wentworth. "They beat his head in and knifed him in a dozen places. We ain't found the girl—nothing but part of her dress he was hanging onto. That makes ten girls disappeared. Not a sign of them left or the dirty dogs that snatched them."

"Ghastly!" Kirkpatrick muttered, as he came up beside Wentworth and gazed down at the sheeted bodies. "There have been complaints about women being annoyed here in the park, for the past couple weeks—but nothing like this! Coming on top of Doctor Sprague's murder, the newspapers will ride me on a rail in the morning."

"Both are tied together, Kirk," Wentworth told him grimly, "the madness curse and this horrible outrage. Half a dozen of your men over in the arsenal were stricken with madness in order that this deviltry could be staged—just the way they got the men outside Sprague's house."

"Half a dozen more!" The commissioner's voice was little more than a hoarse whisper. "But why, Dick—why? Why such an outrage as this one in the park? There's something more behind it—some reason for concentrating our attention here in the darkness—"

Suddenly his jaw dropped and swift fear leaped into his eyes.

"Barry Winant—that's the answer!" he exclaimed. "His hotel is the Parker-Holland—only a short distance from here. This uproar will draw every reserve from that precinct, and the excitement will empty the district of spectators. The devils will be able to do as they please!"

Barry Winant, the special prosecutor... Manny Green's veiled threat flashed back into Wentworth's mind, as he led the way to the street, shouldering a way through the crowd, with Kirkpatrick close at his side. Straight toward his sedan he raced—or toward where his sedan should have been. Now it was gone, the curb empty.

Nita—what had become of her? Wentworth remembered seeing her in the park, just as the stricken policeman collided with him. Was she still in there, perhaps looking for him? Or was she in there because those murdering devils had seized and dragged her out of sight with the other victims of the night's horror?

Wentworth's jaws clenched grimly. But that empty spot at the curb reassured him, told him that she must have come back to the street and driven away. But why and where? Why should she leave him there, and where would she go?

THERE WAS no time to wonder about Nita now, or to race back into the park and search for her—much as he desired to. Kirkpatrick was making a bee-line to one of the police cars, diving in behind the wheel and impatiently holding the door open as he kicked the motor into action. The moment Wentworth stepped on the running-board, the car slipped into gear and tore down the avenue, screaming siren clearing a way through the traffic.

Down the avenue they went, into the side street on which the Parker-Holland was located. As Kirkpatrick had predicted, the street was empty save for a few late-comers, panting as they now raced toward the avenue and the excitement that was drawing thousands.

"We've wasted precious minutes," the commissioner worried. "Ten to one, they've had time to finish him—to leave him the way you found poor Sprague. If they have—"

The grim oath he swore was lost, as he leaped out of the car in front of the fashionable hotel and raced along beneath the canopy to the entrance. Wentworth was less than a step behind him, as he flung through the doorway and sped across the lobby toward the elevators. Yet in Wentworth's brain an alarm-bell was beginning to ring frantically.

Something was wrong, a persistent sixth sense warned him. And then he knew what it was!

The doorman had not been outside at his post as usual! There had been nobody at the curb to open the car door, as they skidded to a stop—nobody to warn them that they could not leave the machine parked there in the main entrance.

"Seventeen-o-two!" Kirkpatrick shouted as he reached the elevator.

The elevator door slid shut behind him so sharply that it would have slammed in Wentworth's face and cut him off—but for the fact that the instinctive warning that had flashed into his brain had not gone unheeded. Both his hands were streaking toward his shoulder holsters, as he dived across the lobby, just in time to side-step a shower of lead that spat at him from a half dozen silenced automatics!

CHAPTER 3
THE PROSECUTION CLOSES

THE LOBBY, Wentworth had noticed in that fractional second, while he darted through Death's groping fingers, was deserted except for the clerks at the desk, the bellhops standing at attention, the operators half-framed in the doors of their cars. Their peculiar immobility—the frozen look on their blanched faces—added an exclamation-point to the warning that had already set his every nerve aquiver. The employees were terrified, standing there, helpless, under the guns of hidden captors!

It was his warning.

The moment Wentworth changed his course toward the elevators, and sprang behind the shimmering bulk of a huge fountain in the center of the lobby, hell broke loose. Bullets spattered against the three bronze maidens who supported a brimming sea-shell above their heads. Crouched in the center, beneath the water-filled shell, Wentworth fired from behind the protection of their metallic bodies, sending his deadly bullets knifing through the falling water that served as an additional shield as it veiled him from the sniping marksmen.

From behind marble pillars, the shelter of large potted plants, through the bars of the cashier's cage and over the top of the reception desk, black-masked faces peered at him and flaming gun muzzles sought him. The crackle of their muffled popping drummed at him from all sides, furnishing a deadly accompaniment to the thunder of his own twin weapons.

"Get him out of there, you lugs!" a harsh voice snarled above the din. "Get him out, or you'll have the cops—" The cry broke off.

That was it—the cops! Those automatics were silenced so that they would not make too much noise or attract attention.

Under the lash of that snarling voice, the killers closed in on the fountain. Heavy lobby chairs started moving forward, mobile fortresses for the gunmen crawling behind them. Wentworth stopped four, but the others were heavy and substantial. His bullets bored into the hard wood but got no farther. At this rate, it would be only seconds now....

In a frenzy of fear, one of the clerks darted from the side of the desk and started on a wild, hopeless dash to the door. Midway across the lobby, bullets tore through him, jerked him upright—then set him sprawling on his face, twitching on the reddening stone floor.

Wentworth's bleak eyes slitted, and he brought down one of the killers—then whirled to send two bullets crashing through the plate-glass windows of the street doors. In a thousand pieces, the splintered glass clattered to the floor and out onto the steps.

For a moment, there was stunned silence in the reverberating lobby, as the gunmen realized what he had done—the effect that crashing glass, tumbling out on the street, was bound to have. Wentworth seized the brief respite to slip fresh clips into his emptied guns. Snarling curses ended that startled truce, and three of the thugs leaped from cover and came on with roaring guns. Others were getting up, following their example. But that meant that the hotel employees were left unguarded, and one of them had his wits about him....

Wentworth saw him duck behind the counter, saw a door behind the desk push inward as the clerk must have crawled through it—and then the lights went out! Only one remained—a dim dome light, an emergency light that illuminated the big lobby, weirdly.

In that uncertain radiance the oncoming killers looked like shadowy gnomes, indistinct phantoms bearing orange death-flowers in their hands. Before they could recover from their surprise, Wentworth had wriggled from his shelter, dived through the veil of water and was behind one of the chairs that had reached half-way to its objective before his bullets put a stop to its progress.

Now there was only the deep roar of his guns to distinguish his position from that of the others. Instead of being able to converge on a trapped victim, they were fighting a deadly marksman who was right there among them, ready to cut them down from any side.

That realization was like a spark to a keg of gunpowder. Wentworth's moving chair bumped into one coming from another direction—a fortress with two startled defenders who swung their weapons around to bear on him too late. One died with

Wentworth's bullet in his throat; the other leaped to his feet with a yell of terror and raced across the lobby—raced desperately to beat his panic-stricken fellows to the rear doors.

Now there were faces at the main entrance, men peering in warily through the shattered doors. People on the street were at last aware of what was going on, and a crowd was gathering. Escape in that direction had become precarious—and the knowledge completed the rout that had been started by that terrified yell.

Running with the fleeing killers, Wentworth lashed out with his weapons, smashing every head that came within his reach as he raced toward the elevators. The lift into which he dashed was empty except for the shuddering operator who cowered in one corner.

Wentworth paid no attention to him but leaped to the controls, himself, and sent the car scooting up to the seventeenth floor. Seventeen-o-two, Kirkpatrick had said. That was a suite at the end of the hall. Wentworth pushed the button and banged on the door, but there was no response or sound from within.

WENTWORTH'S HAND on the knob turned, and he stepped into the private lobby. The lights were lit, but his entrance attracted no attention. Warily, he walked through the suite, room after room, his automatic ready in his hand—but the place was empty. The lit lamps, the position of various pieces of furniture, a half-smoked cigar on a tray—all gave the impression of very recent occupancy. But Barry Winant was gone.

More than that, Winant had gone after a struggle. An overturned chair, a sheaf of scattered papers—one of them ground

31

RICHARD WENTWORTH

into the rug by a rubber heel—told their mute story of a swift battle—of a man overcome before he had been able to put up effective resistance. That was it.

Standing there in the middle of the special prosecutor's living-room, Wentworth sniffed, puzzled. A familiar odor hung over the place, just a suggestion of a perfume that whispered something to him. Somewhere, very recently, he had encountered that delicate fragrance. Somewhere—

And then his eyes flashed to the corner, to Winant's desk and the crumpled ball of white cloth just visible beneath it.

When he had plucked that crumpled wad out from its hiding-place and examined it, he saw that it was a frilly, feminine handkerchief—the initials *AS* in one corner. Alicia Sprague's handkerchief! It was in the Sprague home that he had noticed that elusive fragrance. So Alicia Sprague had been here in Barry Winant's apartment… and been here recently, for the handkerchief was damp….

Wentworth's eyes strayed from the wisp of lace to Winant's desk, its top littered with papers as if the prosecutor had been interrupted in the midst of his work. One of those papers lay squarely in the center, a sheet with a few words printed on it. Affixed to it was some sort of seal—a seal that sent a chill trickle down Wentworth's spine as he recognized it!

The note was typewritten, and not addressed to Barry Winant

but to the world at large. Leaning over the desk, Wentworth read—

WARNING

Let Barry Winant's fate be a lesson to you! The same will be meted out to any who disobey orders or try to interfere with—

In place of a signature, one of those now all too familiar leering soap-relief faces had been affixed to the sheet.

Winant's fate—but *what* was Winant's fate? Had he been kidnaped, dragged off somewhere to be tortured and mutilated? Had he been killed? There was absolutely nothing in the apartment to answer those questions.

Thoughtfully, Wentworth walked back into the hallway and stood for a moment, undecided in the doorway. His sharp ears caught a sound at the other end of the corridor. Quickly, he hot-footed over the carpeted stretch until he came to the door of an elevator—the freight lift. The indicator showed that it was coming up. Thirteenth floor, fourteenth, fifteenth—

Wentworth set himself, alertly balanced on the balls of his feet, his muscles tensed, ready to spring, an automatic gripped at his side. The elevator was at the fifteenth floor—inner gate pushed back—and then the door opened.

As it drew back, he caught a glimpse of two husky thugs, one at the controls, the other at the side of the doorway. Before he could blaze away at them, Barry Winant staggered into the opening. Groping his way like a drunken man, he lurched out into the corridor, his sharp-featured, intelligent face twisted in an inane grin!

Flame belched at Wentworth from the maw of the elevator. A bullet whined by his ear; another tore at his coat. For a moment he was at a disadvantage, unable to fire because Winant had blundered into his way. Then his gun blazed, and one of the thugs pitched head-foremost as he leaped out into the hallway. But the other sprang from behind Winant, and his gun barrel lashed out at Wentworth's head.

Wentworth managed to dodge that blow, but the muzzle caught him in the neck, smashed down with such force that it seemed to tear right through the flesh and bone. White-hot agony stabbed through him as he staggered back against the wall, covering his head with his left arm. Again, that heavy gun swung up for a skull-crushing blow....

Desperately, he tried to lift his right arm. It seemed paralyzed from the shoulder down to the fingertips. His muscles would not obey his will and the whole limb seemed detached. Frantically, he strained, and excruciating pain was his reward—but the arm lifted. Like a dead thing he saw it raise, saw his finger squeeze on the trigger though he could not feel his muscles contracting.

The gun roared—and the thug yelped with pain as he clutched at his side. That seemed to have taken an eternity... yet it must have been no more than a few seconds. The gunman's down-swinging arm was caught in mid-arc. His pain made him forget his savage rage; made him slump back against the elevator and pull himself into it.

He was going to get away. Wentworth knew that he must be stopped. But when he tried to thrust himself into the elevator doorway his body seemed to move with the deliberateness of a slow-motion movie. Before he could reach the door, it slid shut, and then he heard the whirr of machinery as it started downward....

IT SEEMED hours that he leaned there against the closed door, fighting himself, battling frenziedly to cast off the lethargy that enveloped him—and at last he succeeded. Strength flowed back into his limbs like a scalding stream. His whole body tingled, prickled agonizingly—but he could move!

Carefully, he worked at the closed shaft door, pushing and tugging at it. The wounded thug had not closed it completely; there was barely sufficient room to insert a pencil between it and the jamb. Wentworth chose a long skeleton key, got it into the aperture and worked the latch upward until he could lift it clear and swing the door back.

Looking down the deep shaft, he could see that the elevator was at the bottom. Voices came up to him indistinctly. They were still down there; there was yet time.

Swinging out into the shaft, he grasped the cable and tightened his legs around it, clung grimly as his hands started to slip. The grease with which it was coated was treacherous stuff. Once he started plummeting downward, that cable would burn through his clothing and sear its way into his body like a knife.

Hand under hand, he worked his way downward, braking himself tensely whenever he started to slip, fighting back the mad desire to shoot to the bottom before those murdering devils had time to escape. Past the main floor and down to the basement—and then his feet touched the top of the car. His fingers found the trap, lifted it, and he dropped down into the car itself.

The door stood open, and, through it, he caught a glimpse of a van-like truck that stood in the service driveway behind the hotel. Half a dozen thugs were clustered around its back door. Two of them were lifting something to others who stood in the van, reaching down to receive it.

That "something" was Stanley Kirkpatrick's limp body!

Like machine-gun bullets, Wentworth's automatics poured their slugs into that knot of thugs. The one in the doorway of the van yelped and pitched backward into the dark interior. One of those who grasped Kirkpatrick howled in agony; the other spun crazily and dropped to the street. Remorselessly, Wentworth pulled his triggers—and the killers melted away before his gun muzzles. Frantically, they piled into the van and yanked the doors closed. Over the commissioner's body, Wentworth crouched, trying to drive his slugs into the driver's compartment. But the window was up, and he suspected it was made of bullet-proof glass.

With a roaring backfire, the van sped out onto the street. Wentworth was close behind it, as it cleared the curb, but there was no sort of vehicle at hand with which he could pursue. Helplessly, he had to watch it fade down the block and disappear around a corner....

KIRKPATRICK WAS reviving, when Wentworth staggered back into the hotel. The police had come down into the basement and carried him inside and up to the lobby. They were working over him there under the direction of an officious little individual in evening clothes whom Wentworth recognized as Deputy Commissioner Harvey Newell.

Newell, whose honorary title had been secured for him through political influence, obviously revelled in this opportunity to bask in the temporary authority he had taken upon himself. Busily, he fussed about the lobby, issuing orders and cross-questioning the hotel employees who had witnessed the gun battle.

"It seems that the entire hotel was in the control of a band of thieves for nearly fifteen minutes," he announced to the newspapermen who were following him around. "The most daring exhibition of brigandage New York has ever known! By overpowering the employees, they were able to block every door and take over the telephone switchboard so that all chance of communicating with the outside world was cut off. Meanwhile, they looted the hotel safe and robbed scores of guests of their money and jewels."

One of the reporters wanted to know how Newell happened to be on hand so opportunely, and he rose readily to the bait.

"I was a guest at the dinner-dance sponsored by Aaron Fairchild," he explained. "Our first intimation of the state of affairs came when we were confronted by machine guns that covered us from the balcony of the ballroom. We had no choice but to submit, while masked thieves circulated among us and relieved us of our valuables. The loss from that hold-up alone will run into hundreds of thousands of dollars."

That was no exaggeration, Wentworth knew. Aaron Fairchild was one of the city's socialites—member of a family whose financial influence was felt throughout the nation. The annual dinner-dance he sponsored was an elaborate, aristocratic affair at which the city's blue-bloods vied in the attempt to outshine one another—a veritable paradise for a band of jewel thieves.

So far as he could judge, Wentworth estimated that there must have been no less than twenty-five or thirty of the raiders, but none of them had been caught and the only evidence that remained were the corpses of four—and the living corpses of four detectives who, like Barry Winant, had joined the brainless legion of the lost men.

"Four more of Manny Green's hoodlums," Kirkpatrick confided when he was back on his feet and had had a look at the bodies. "Well known thugs, all of them—and all no doubt under orders from Manny's brother Solly. That's the answer to this series of outrages, Dick—an outburst of lawlessness to demonstrate that Manny Green can't be kept behind bars. But we're going to show him that he can. The moment I get back to headquarters, I'm sending out a round-up call for Solly. Before I'm finished, I'll have every member of his rotten mob on his way up the river—or under six feet of sod."

All the way downtown, he fumed over the brazenness of the night's deviltry. But as Wentworth listened, he knew that much of the commissioner's bluster was camouflage, a smokescreen raised to conceal his fear. Kirkpatrick was badly scared because he was fighting something that he did not understand—something striking at the very heart of the department.

And Wentworth did not blame him. It took no second-sight

to see the menace that hung over the metropolis. One glance into the eyes of those terrified officers was sufficient to envision a police force shackled by fear, a city prostrate under the ruthless domination of a criminal horde that was secure in the assurance that it could not be curbed!

But there was one who would dare fight back—no matter how terrifying the fate with which he was threatened. More than once the Spider had taken a hand in the game when the police were helplessly checkmated. This time, he would take up the gage of battle before the department, that was Kirkpatrick's pride, had been hopelessly undermined and wrecked by cancerous fear....

How real was that danger was demonstrated the moment they walked into the commissioner's office.

KIRKPATRICK STRODE to his desk, plopped down vigorously in his chair and reached for his phone. Then he halted, hand halfway to the instrument. Unbelievingly his amazed eyes stared down at a typewritten message on a sheet of paper, similar to the one that had been lying on Barry Winant's desk, and which read—

WARNING

The fate of New York City is in your hands. If you have the interests of the city at heart, as you profess, resign! Every hour that you hang onto the commissionership will cost the city thousands of dollars—and the police department hundreds of lives! This is the ultimatum of—

And again, glued to the paper, in lieu of a signature, was a fiendishly realistic soap model of an insanely grinning face!

Kirkpatrick's face was choleric as he took the note back from Wentworth and stared at it. His square jaw was grim. His fingers clasped and unclasped over the arms of his chair, before he reached for the phone and barked a summons for the specialists now working over the madness victims brought in from Central Park.

"Resign?" he growled wrathfully, as he waited for the physicians to come to the office. "Resign so that they can smash the department like an army without a leader? I'll give them all the resignation they're looking for! Once we discover how this deviltry is accomplished."

But that, unfortunately, seemed as remote as when the first victim lost his sanity.

The moment the two experts, who had been summoned to police headquarters, stepped into the office, Wentworth knew what they would report. Their puzzled faces delivered their verdict.

"These cases are amazing," the spokesman said slowly. "If I did not know that these men had been perfectly sane a few hours ago, I should take them for mental cases of long standing. The derangement is so complete that all the faculties have been affected except that of locomotion—and even over that there seems to be little control."

"What caused it, Doctor?" Kirkpatrick interrupted impatiently. "How can I protect the rest of my men from it? That's what I want to know."

"So far as we have been able to determine, they have been subjected to a terrific shock which has disorganized the entire nervous system and dislodged all reason," the physician pronounced hesitantly. "To find out how that was accomplished is a task for your detectives, not for us. We can only tell you what the result has been—and what it is likely to be. The condition may, of course, improve and gradually disappear. But, from present manifestations, the men give every indication of incurable insanity."

Wentworth felt a chill stealing into his heart, as he thought of those men, strong and in the prime of life, suddenly plunged into mental darkness that would hang over them until the grave! The man who could heartlessly decree such a fate for his fellows was a monster for whom even death was too merciful a punishment!

The chill stole deeper, when Wentworth's thoughts flashed to Nita. Where was she? As soon as he reached headquarters, he tried to get her by telephone. But there had been no answer at her apartment and she had not been in touch with his Sutton Place residence where there was always someone waiting to receive a message. Was it possible that she had fallen into the hands of that heartless devil?

"Sergeant Mulroy," Kirkpatrick was talking to the operator. "Is he still out there? Send him in." Then, as he turned back to Wentworth, "Mulroy is the man you saw smashed up on Central Park West. He seemed out of his head for a while, but he's come around all right. Perhaps he knows what happened to Connors, who was driving him."

Mulroy was "all right" so far as sanity was concerned, but he was a shaken man—whose pasty face and nervous eyes were those of one who had been cast into hell and then miraculously snatched out again. His hands and his lips twitched continually, when he sank into the chair beside Kirkpatrick's desk and faced the commissioner.

"I don't rightly know what happened, sir," he murmured uncertainly, when Kirkpatrick asked for his story. "Everything's sort o' hazy. I remember, though, I was feelin' queer just before the accident—the blood in my head poundin' and churnin' like the water in one o' them washin' machines. It got so bad that I opened the door and stuck my head out to cool off. That's what I was doin' when the call come over the radio—and then we had the accident."

"Why?" Kirkpatrick prompted. "How did the car get out of control? Wasn't Connors well?"

"He didn't say nothin' to me, sir." The sergeant shook his head. "He seemed all right. We was just cruisin' along slow until the call come in—and then we started rollin' all over the street. I looked at Connors and he was grinnin' like a drunk—grinnin' and gibberin' like an idiot. It gives me the creeps even to think about it!"

"Whatever it is that causes these seizures, it seems able to strike anywhere," Kirkpatrick summed up after Mulroy had left. "Men patrolling their beats, riding in cars, in the station houses. A policeman doesn't seem to be safe anywhere—and that's what the men are whispering. The uncertainty, the constant menace, is fraying their nerves and demoralizing them—"

The telephone interrupted him, and Wentworth noticed his

apprehensive start before he reached for the instrument. Not only were the nerves of the men fraying under this ordeal; their commissioner was on hair-trigger, jumpy as a cat.

"It's for you, Dick." He backed away to make room at the desk. "Nita calling you."

Nita! Wentworth's pulses leaped and he grabbed up the receiver, thrilled as her voice came to him over the wire. She was all right; she was safe and out of the danger he had hardly dared to think about….

"I COULDN'T call you before, Dick," she apologized. I've been tied up—tied up in the back of the car—for what seemed like hours. That girl and young fellow you helped in the park— they tied me up and put a gag in my mouth so that I couldn't scream, and then left me in the back of the car." She paused.

"Yes, I let them hide in the car when I saw that you wanted them to escape," she answered his surprised suggestion. "I drove through the police line without being stopped, and, as soon as they were safe, they took the car away from me. When I managed to get loose, I drove back to the Towers—and when I got up to my apartment, Olga didn't know me. She's a raving maniac, Dick! She just wanders in and out of the rooms talking to herself and laughing in a way that chills my blood! I've already sent for an ambulance to take her away.

"What is this thing that is coming over people, Dick?" she half-sobbed. "It's the work of the same person who killed Doctor Sprague, I know, for one of those horrible leering soap faces was stuck to the front of the clock on my mantelpiece!"

One of those damning soap faces above her mantelpiece!

Then the doom that had overtaken Olga, the maid, had been meant for Nita! She had escaped this time, but the fiend would not be stopped so easily. He would strike again—and the next time he would not miss!

"Get out of that apartment, Nita," Wentworth decided quickly. "Get out just as soon as the ambulance comes for Olga. God knows what sort of deviltry went on there while you were away—but if they could get in once they can get in again. Pack a bag and check in at the Raleigh. Use the Mary Cordova name, and I'll call you later tonight."

CHAPTER 4
DANCE OF DEATH

THE BACKS of Wentworth's hands were damp with perspiration, as he dropped the instrument back into its cradle and told Kirkpatrick what had happened. Nita was in danger—there was no possible doubt of that. She was in appalling danger, but to go to her now would be of little avail. That might only lead the killers to her hotel hideout, if they were shadowing him.

The most effective way to defend her would be to track down this murdering monster and scotch him like the poisonous snake that he was. To track him down....

The girl in the park! She might be the answer to that. Unless she was tied up with this murder gang, why had she been there in the park when those outrages were being perpetrated? Why had she and the young fellow, who was with her, been so anxious to escape without being seen by the police? Why had they overpowered Nita? Why had they left her tied up so that she could not get home until Olga had been driven mad?

The answers to those questions were to be found in the heart of the slums—in that odorous rabbit-warren of narrow streets and dingy tenements that lies east of the Bowery. And they could be found not by Richard Wentworth, but by the man who was known there as—Blinky McQuade.

Wentworth glanced at his watch. It was almost eleven o'clock, but there still was plenty of time if he hurried. A block from police headquarters, he hailed a cab and was driven to within a block of his destination. The rest of the way he would go on foot, for the residents of Holian Alley were not addicted to cab-riding. To be driven up to the door would only attract attention he very much desired to avoid.

The last house on Holian Alley, where it joined with Pallin Place to form the base of a V, was Number One. A disreputable-looking, four-story tenement, on a noisome, squalid street, it merged with its neighbors in drab ugliness—just as its shifty-eyed, furtive-looking denizens mingled in the obscurity of poverty. It was an ideal location for the shambling individual who lived on the second floor, rear. Ideal, because he could come and go without interference or questions being asked; because the little court, that was the back yard for Number One, and also for the corresponding building on Pallin Place, afforded an entrance and exit through both buildings—a fact of which the tenants of both took frequent advantage.

The tenant of that second floor, rear, was known to his underworld associates as 'Blinky McQuade.' Years ago, they said, he had been a swaggering safe-blower—until a premature explosion almost ended his career and left his eyes so weak that he had to wear powerful glasses with metallic hoods over the lenses. An insignificant-appearing, round-shouldered hanger-on of the underworld, he was tolerated because his fingers, trained by necessity, could open a safe as efficiently as the nitroglycerin he had formerly used.

Into Blinky McQuade's room Wentworth let himself with a key. Quietly, he stepped to the courtyard window and drew the shade back, carefully. A light was burning in the room in the Pallin Place building that came together with his, to make the sharp point of the V, and Wentworth nodded with satisfaction.

The occupant of that room was Catherine O'Keefe, a pretty, clean-looking girl of about twenty whose face made no secret of her Irish ancestry. Blue-eyed and red-haired, there was a freshness, a wholesomeness to her face, that made her seem oddly out of place in that dreary back-slough of humanity. Wentworth had wondered what she was doing down there in the slums—and tonight seemed to supply his answer.

Catherine O'Keefe was the girl he had seen cowering away from the police in Central Park.

He had known her at once, but she had not recognized him—

nor would anyone have recognized slovenly Blinky McQuade in the suave, well poised and perfectly tailored Richard Wentworth. Yet the two were one and the same—and, even as Wentworth stood there at the courtyard window, he was taking off his garments to change into the well worn and unpressed outfit that was Blinky's.

Blinky McQuade was Wentworth's underworld personality, a character he had brought into being and established there in the slums so that he might have access to criminal haunts and underworld rendezvous closed to any but the initiate. Places where Richard Wentworth could not have gained admittance, where the police never penetrated, where even the Spider could have blasted his way only with flaming guns—Blinky was welcome.

Since Blinky had taken up his spasmodic residence here in Holian Alley, he had owed escape from capture and death on more than one occasion to Catherine O'Keefe and her handy apartment so close to his own. That was why he had instinctively gone to her rescue when the police cordon was closing around her. But if she was part of the devilish combine, waging this criminal war with insanity as its frightful weapon, there could be no mercy or clemency for her.

THE BOTTOM of her window was raised a few inches above the sill. By leaning out of his own window with a cane, he was able to push back her drawn shade sufficiently so that he could see into a part of the room. She was there, sitting on the edge of her bed, talking earnestly to a man who faced her on a chair—a man Wentworth recognized as her companion of the park.

"Please, Ed, I don't want you to go—I'm afraid," she was pleading with him, as she clung to his sleeve. "The police may be after you now, and if you are caught—"

Wentworth didn't wait for any more. Hurrying over to the mammoth-sized bed, that was the principal article of furniture in the shabby room, he knelt in the center of it. Then he pressed his fingers against the secret springs concealed in the massive headboard. They released a panel. Noiselessly, it opened out and became a completely equipped make-up shelf in front of a brightly lighted mirror.

Screening the light so that it could not be seen from the window, Wentworth went to work. Rapidly, his skilled fingers applied skin lotion, make-up pencil and greasepaint. A prepared pad went into his mouth to make his lower lip pendulous; a few moments of work on his hair transformed it into a rumpled, gray-streaked mop; the hooded spectacles went into place—and then he was ready for the ragged clothes that would complete his metamorphosis.

But, as his flying fingers worked, his ears were straining to catch every sound from the room opposite.

Catherine was sobbing. He heard the chair scrape back over the floor, as the man rose and started toward the door.

"Please," she begged again, "it's too much of a chance, Ed. It isn't worth it—not to take such a chance of being caught. You know what it will mean, if the police grab you."

"They won't," Ed bit off determinedly. "Don't worry, Cath—I

AARON
FAIRCHILD

HARVEY NEWELL

VICTOR HANSON

ALICIA
SPRAGUE

50

CATHARINE O'KEEFE

EDWARD EMMET

DANIEL DALEY

can take care of myself—I *have* to go through with it—you know that. I'm not going to back down now when I've gone this far—"

Wentworth heard him walking toward the door, heard the girl's last fervent protest—and then her heart-broken sobs as the door opened and quickly closed. Her companion had gone... and, a few moments later, Blinky McQuade slipped out of his door and hurried down the stairs to the murk of "Holy Alley."

The street, he noticed, was unusually deserted and quiet— so still that, drawn back deep into the shadowy doorway of Number One, he had no difficulty picking up the sound of Ed's footsteps as he came down Pallin Place and started toward the avenue. Blinky followed at a discreet distance—and then quickened his pace when he saw that the young fellow was about to hail an uptown bus.

They boarded it together, and Blinky slumped into a seat from which he could watch the younger man. About twenty-five, he seemed to be—a husky young fellow with ruddy cheeks and grayish eyes. Nervously, he drummed one foot on the floor and glanced at the watch that was strapped to his wrist. Twice he took out a cigarette and put it back into the package as he glared out of the window.

Blinky could fairly see his mental processes operating—could see him hesitating, then goading himself with grim determination.

At Forty-second Street, he got out and took a crosstown car, and his slouching shadow followed him—followed until they arrived at a large dance hall on the West Side. There the youth paced up and down nervously, while Blinky merged into the black doorway of a near-by store.

Five minutes, Ed kept that uneasy vigil, and then another figure came swaggering up the street—a rakishly dressed individual who, despite his strutting, walked with the lithe grace of a jungle cat. The moment he strode within the rays of a street-light, Blinky recognized him as Joe Tobin, a quick-triggered killer.

"You here, eh?" Blinky heard Tobin greet Ed, as the young fellow stepped forward to meet him. "Didn't think you'd have the guts to show up—an' I still don't think you got what it takes to go through with it. But you'll have plenty o' chance...."

Then they were out of earshot, going through the doorway and upstairs to the dancehall on the second floor.

A FEW minutes later, Blinky followed them, paid a half-dollar admission, and walked into a gaudily decorated ballroom. It reeked with tobacco smoke and was packed with dancers gyrating in time to the blaring discords of a so-called swing band. The place was stuffy and poorly ventilated, and the dancers were, for the most part, impecunious young fellows with not more than a few dollars in their pockets and girls whose only adornments were a few items of costume jewelry.

Blinky mentally contrasted the cheap layout with the elegant Fairchild dinner-dance at the Parker-Holland Hotel—and wondered. Joe Tobin was in that place for no good, yet what could have brought him there? Robbery of the Fairchild dance was easily understandable, but to hold up this crowded hall would not be worth the time of a real self-respecting thug.

Unobtrusively, Blinky made his way around the edge of the dance floor, his spectacled eyes keenly alert for anything in the slightest way suspicious. Twice he saw faces he recognized— cruel, vulpine faces that he had seen before in haunts where only criminals gather yet, like the rest, they seemed to be absorbed with their dancing partners.

There was nothing suspicious—until suddenly angry words rose above the strident notes of the orchestra. Then came shrill feminine screams. The dancers were slowing their steps, necks craning inquisitively; men were leaving their partners, hurrying to where the crowd was deepening at one side of the hall. Blinky caught a glimpse of waving fists. Obscene curses ripped through the sudden quiet that had come over the place as the musicians paused with their instruments still in their hands.

"Let him have it, Barney!" someone yelled—and bodies thudded to the floor in a wild scuffle.

Blinky was trying to worm his way through the crowd, when the first shots rang out—two in quick succession, followed by a moan of agony and a woman's hysterical shriek. For a moment, those were the only sounds in the unnatural stillness. Then guns started barking from every corner of the hall. Blinky saw the orange flashes, as bullets poured into the terrified crowd. Women turned and tried to fight their way through the dense jam behind them, while men, wild with panic, flailed right and left with their fists as they now struggled madly to escape.

In less than a minute, that laughing crowd had become a milling mob of wild-eyed people whose only thought was to fight their way to safety. Men went down under that rain of bullets. Women tried hopelessly to get them to their feet. They were bowled over by the surging crowd, trampled to the floor, their screams of agony mingling with the moans of the bullet-torn victims who writhed beside them.

Half a dozen times, Blinky grabbed girls and held them on their feet just in time to save them from going down. A dozen times, he smashed his fists into the faces of frenzied men to batter them back to their senses. But there was no stemming that mad panic.

Slowly, he gave ground and tried to work his way out of the thick of the jam. Then he caught a glimpse of Ed; he saw the youth with a revolver in his hand, firing over the heads of the roaring crowd, his face a grim, white mask with bulging, desperate eyes. In the same instant, Blinky saw Joe Tobin, farther back. The killer's gun blazed as his lips curled away from his teeth in a wolfish snarl—then the gun muzzle swung around and deliberately centered on Ed's back!

One instant, Blinky was unarmed; the next an automatic was in his right hand, its muzzle spurting flame as its roar contributed to the din—and Tobin's weapon went spinning from his hand. Amazed, he stared unbelievingly at his empty hand—then began to massage his tingling fingers, as a flood of vile curses poured from his snarling lips.

Savagely, he glared around him. For a fraction of a second, his eyes fastened on Blinky, held there uncertainly—and then the whole building shuddered and seemed ready to come down as a terrific explosion shook it to its foundation. A lurid burst of light—then clouds of smoke and the acrid odor of burned gunpowder. Blinky saw bodies hurled into the air, pinioned momentarily against the glare of the explosion. Then the lights went out, and the only illumination in that ghastly shambles was what trickled feebly through the curtained windows....

JUST BEFORE the blast, Blinky had located the nearest door. Now he fought his way to it through the pack of bodies that writhed and battled blindly in the darkness. Ahead was a rectangle of light from the hallway—but, before he reached it, the rectangle narrowed and then disappeared entirely as the door slammed shut. Outside, a key turned in the lock. Then bullets came tearing through the panels to drive back the throng that was beating against it with impotent fists.

The place was a death-trap! Locked in, penned up, worse than rats, that throng of innocent and unsuspecting merry-makers had been condemned to a horrible death! Their screams rose to a new crescendo as they began to realize that escape was cut off. The dread cry of "Fire!" rang out above the din! Red tongues began to lick up one of the walls, casting a wavering crimson half-light over the terror-distorted faces!

Hundreds of innocent people callously doomed to horrible slaughter! Wentworth's soul writhed, as he realized the ghastly enormity of the thing he was witnessing. Grimly, he vowed to see that the fiend, who had ordained this atrocity, suffered for every life now snuffed out.

What was the purpose of this needless slaughter? What could the inhuman devil hope to gain by this heartless massacre of a mob of simple, inoffensive people? Those questions were churning through Wentworth's mind, as he fought his way back from the locked door and at last reached a cleared space. But the answer was not here in this seething charnel-house, unless it could be dragged from the lips of the youth he knew as Ed. Blinky caught sight of him, blundering blindly through the mob, frantic as any of the innocent victims.

Instantly, Blinky made a dive for him, reached his side and grabbed him by an arm—just as the sound of police sirens came through the shattered windows, an eerie wail above that raging inferno.

"Come on—we gotta get out o' here!" he yelled in the young fellows ear. "If the cops find that rod on you—"

"I threw it away," the youth gasped, but the mention of police had thrown him into fresh panic.

Unresisting, he followed as Blinky dragged him toward the back of the hall, then led the way along the wall until he located a door that opened onto a pantry, which, in turn, led out to the kitchen. The stoves gleamed redly in the darkness, but the kitchen was deserted, the cook and waiters long since flown.

At the farther end, Blinky located a door that opened onto a narrow hallway and a stairs leading down to the employees' entrance. Police cars were already gliding up to the curb nearer to the corner, as they opened the door and slipped into the street. Policemen were piling out, running toward the main entrance, while others began to push back the crowd already clogging the street.

Like a ferret, Blinky dodged in among the spectators, Ed at his heels. For a moment, curious eyes turned on them and men yelled. Then they were lost in the crowd, blanketed by the wave of spectators whom the police were pushing back with nightsticks.

Gradually, Blinky led the way back, worming a path to the rear until they were at the fringe of the crowd—and then off down the avenue. Not until then did he have a chance to turn to his white-faced companion.

"You—you got me out of that," the youth gulped. "If you hadn't taken hold of me, I'd be back there yet. I—I appreciate that. My name is Ed—Ed Emmet."

"Looks like your pals ducked out an' left you holdin' the bag, don't it, Emmet?" Blinky hazarded, his face twisted into a know-ing grin.

Emmet gulped before he answered. Then he took the plunge. "I don't know anything about that—back there," he lied. "I went up there to the Golden Palace to meet a friend. I didn't have any idea what would happen—"

"That's why you packed your rod along, I suppose?" Blinky observed dryly. "That's why you was takin' pot-shots at the crowd?"

"I—I picked that gun up from the floor," the youth stammered. "I was firing over their heads—so help me God, that's the truth! I didn't shoot anybody. I was just trying to scare them off—to clear a space around me so that I wouldn't be knocked down and trampled."

"All right, bud; have it your way," Blinky shrugged, but his keen eyes were probing the lad's face. What he saw there told him that further questioning just then would be useless.

Either Emmet didn't trust him, or else the lad was afraid to say anything which might be construed as squealing. He would keep a closed mouth no matter what pressure was brought to bear on him. But when the proper time came he would talk—Blinky had no doubt about that....

THEY WERE three blocks from the wrecked dancehall when Blinky suddenly stopped and listened. His alert ears had caught the sound of distant shots and then the shrill squeal of a police whistle—coming not from behind them, but from farther to the west.

He had suspected that the dancehall riot might be a cover-up for something more lucrative, but there seemed to be nothing in that shabby neighborhood worth robbing. No banks, wealthy residences or stores with especially valuable merchandise.

The siren of an approaching police car cut short his speculation. Up from downtown it sped, and then swung into the cross-street with reckless abandon. Blinky shot a glance at his companion, expecting to see him dart for cover. Instead, Emmet's face glowed with excitement. He did not run away from the police car, but started to *pursue* it!

Blinky was close at his side, as they raced along the street. Ahead, the police car had swung back into the middle of the street after that sweeping, two-wheel turn—but now was veering crazily, zigzagging toward the corner. There it crashed into an elevated pillar and burst into flames.

Blinky gave the wreckage only a cursory glance, as he and Emmet ran past. It revealed the mangled bodies of two officers dangling from it, as if they had been hurled out of the cab by the crash. The moment he rounded the corner, Blinky discovered the cause of the trouble.

Across the way was an armory, dark and apparently deserted, but the doors were open, and a number of still figures lay ominously hunched on the sidewalk. In front of the building were half a dozen van-like trucks—now being loaded with arms and ammunition relayed from the armory as fast as a chain of thugs could carry them.

The armory was being raided, its armament seized by the underworld dictator who had heartlessly decreed that dancehall massacre as a blind so that he might arm his horde for their war against society!

Alert gunmen stood beside the vans, unholstered weapons ready to cut down any passer-by foolhardy enough to offer interference. Emmet paid no attention to them. Recklessly, he ran across the street, Blinky McQuade at his heels.

Shots blazed at them, but the sheer unexpectedness of that unarmed charge made the killers hesitate, the majority holding their fire until they were sure what it was all about.

"Joe! Joe Tobin!" Emmet shouted—and the threatening gun muzzles lowered as the guards turned to the killer who stood in the entrance.

For an instant, Tobin's mean face twisted into an evil, sardonic grin and his own weapon raised. Then he caught sight of Blinky, and his expression changed unfathomably.

"All right—they're okay," he gave the word, and the newcomers were permitted to run through the deadly cordon.

Now that he had a closer look at the sweating thugs who were lugging machine guns and boxes of ammunition out of the looted armory, Blinky recognized several of the hard-eyed killers seen in the dancehall. Evidently, this coup had been timed to perfection. As soon as the dancehall had been thrown into an uproar, those devils had quit the place and hurried over here to help their mates carry out the second part of the program. Even that doomed police car had been mysteriously taken care of so that there would be no possible chance for interference....

"Get in line and help load," ordered a burly thug, who seemed to be superintending the raid, and Blinky and Emmet took their places in the stream of sweating packers.

Up the steps, and past the still bodies of murdered guardsmen, they filed. They went across the wide drill floor and down to the arsenal now nearly emptied, to be given a load and start back to the vans. Like clockwork, that raid proceeded. The moment the vans were filled, the thugs who had been loading them clambered in, and the doors slid shut. Only two vans were left, when Tobin nodded to Emmet and McQuade.

"In you go," he ordered, and they climbed in, to find seats on the piled-up boxes that half-filled the interior.

Curiously, Blinky glanced around at the inside. The narrow gun-slits in the walls needed no explanation. But he was puzzled by a pair of straps and buckles fastened near the ceiling. Before he had time to examine them more closely, the door slid shut and the van was in the darkness except for the dim radiance shed by a dome-light.

At last, Wentworth congratulated himself, he had penetrated the mob. He was on the trail of the monster who signed himself only with a leering idiot face. Undoubtedly, this truck would take him to their headquarters—perhaps to the vicious master criminal himself....

But when he glanced around the van at his fellows, he saw that half a dozen rat-faced killers were watching him suspiciously; guns were trained on him. And, from his position against the door, Joe Tobin eyed him with an expression of evil satisfaction!

CHAPTER 5
DEVIL IN A MURDER MASK

WHEN THE van door opened and the thugs filed out, Wentworth found that they were in a warehouse, the trucks drawn up against the loading platform and the corrugated iron doors pulled down behind them. That warehouse proved to be a veritable arsenal—a barracks for the scum of the underworld. Thieves and hoodlums of every description were there by the dozens, a motley assemblage that eyed him suspiciously—and with an air of anticipation that he could not miss.

The moment the trucks were unloaded Blinky was taken by the arm and escorted down a passageway and up a flight of stairs to a barn-like room roughly fitted up as an office. Behind a battered, flat-top desk sat a pudgy, lowering-faced individual whom he recognized as Solly Green, brother of the convicted Manny.

Joe Tobin stood at the desk beside him. The moment Blinky entered, both turned toward him. Solly's murky eyes peered out from beneath heavy lids, and he frowned heavily. Blinky could see at once that he was ill at ease.

"Here he is," Tobin sneered. "He calls himself Blinky McQuade, and thinks he sneaked in with us without being noticed. He's a rotten stool pigeon the cops tried to plant here." He waited for a reply.

Green's pudgy fingers drummed nervously on the desk-top. At the mention of the police, he stiffened.

"Yeah, he thinks he's mighty cute, and we're all a lot of blind clucks," Tobin's nasty sneer became malevolent. "But we can see, too, wise guy—even if we don't wear cheaters like yours. I saw you take that shot at me in the Golden Palace. Get that gun from under his arm, you men!" he shouted to the others who had crowded into the room.

Before Wentworth could move, his arms were pinned behind him and his guns snatched from their shoulder holsters.

"We got a way of taking care of spies here," Tobin snarled. "When I'm done with you, you won't do any more snooping—unless you come back and haunt the place. Now, you dirty rat!"

Green started to protest, as Tobin leaped past him, but, at a glance from the enraged killer, he subsided and watched with fascinated eyes.

The others, Wentworth noticed, had drawn back against the walls, forming a rough circle that enclosed him and Tobin. Then he realized what he faced—a grim duel to the death such as the pirates of old utilized to settle their differences.

Tobin's hulking body seemed a feline thing as he came forward, half-crouched, a bundle of wiry muscles tensed to spring. Lithely, he circled his intended victim, watching for an opening—and then he had it. Fairly hurling himself forward, he leaped at Blinky, his right fist sweeping up from the floor in a vicious uppercut.

The watching thugs buzzed with excitement—and then gaped in amazement. For, instead of Blinky going down, it was Tobin who staggered back across the room, blood streaming from his nose—the result of a blow so swift that none had seen it!

That blow was a mistake, Wentworth told himself. He must take things easier, seem to have more difficulty evading Tobin's rushes. One of the keener-eyed thieves would be certain to notice that his strength and dexterity were out of all keeping with the broken-down individual Blinky McQuade pretended to be.

But when Tobin came charging in again, the odds had changed materially. In his right hand he clutched a wicked-looking knife, stiletto-pointed and razor-sharp. Before Wentworth could sidestep, it caught the arm of his coat and slit it from shoulder to elbow. Snarling like an enraged beast, Tobin crowded in, knife arm weaving, the deadly point seeking a sheath in Wentworth's body. Twice it nicked his flesh and drew blood before he could tie up the fellow's arm. That blood seemed to whet Tobin's appetite, to drive him utterly mad, as he hurled himself forward for what he intended to be the death-stroke.

Wentworth saw him coming, saw the blade whipping down savagely at his chest—and in that vital moment he went into action. In, under the knife-arm, he ducked, and when Tobin's blade completed its arc it met only air. Before he could recover and draw back for another attempt, his arm shot up into the air, poised there for a moment at a crazy angle—then snapped back sickeningly, as his shoulder popped out of its socket.

Beads of sweat seeped out on Tobin's face, as he writhed in agony. He twisted backward in a desperate effort to break that terrible grip—but Wentworth gave him no relief. Relentlessly, he put on the pressure, until the killer began to howl with pain.

That was too much for his fellows. Too late Wentworth saw

one of them crowd close, saw him whip out a gun and shove it into Tobin's free hand. Tobin's finger tightened on the trigger—and the gun roared deafeningly. Burned powder scorched Wentworth's cheek, and the bullet whistled past his ear. Tobin's finger was crooking again. Wentworth had to release him, grab his gun-wrist and push it back desperately. The pain-maddened killer put every ounce of his bull strength into forcing that gun down into position for the death shot.

Again the room was buzzing with excitement. The watchers were crowding closer, urging Tobin, "Let him have it"—when the door opened and a newcomer stepped into the room.

"Stop it!" he commanded in a hollow voice peculiarly reverberating. "Stop it! Drop that gun, Tobin. Green—you know my rules about fighting."

Toe Tobin's straining muscles relaxed, and Blinky saw the animal rage in the depths of his eyes simmer down into bleak, cold hatred. The surrounding watchers drew back, and through them strode a tall, black-robed figure wearing a mask that covered his entire head. The top and back of that mask were a sickly, grayish white, and the front was a counterpart of the maniacal leer that had become a talisman of madness!

SOLLY SLUMPED back in his chair and tried to avoid the eyes that glared at him from the slits in that crazily grinning mask. His heavy-featured face was sullen, but Wentworth saw that he was mortally afraid.

"What is the meaning of this?" boomed resonantly from behind the mask. "What was this fight about?"

For an instant, silence. Then—

"This is the fate that I mete out to all traitors!"

"This feller—" Solly thumbed toward Blinky—"he's a spy, a louse of a stool pigeon. Tobin caught him—"

"Who are you?" the mask turned toward Blinky. "You just heard what you've been called. What have you got to say for yourself?"

"Blinky McQuade," Wentworth mumbled "I ain't no stool-pigeon, and I c'n prove it. Maybe I did get in here a bit irreg'lar—but I got wind of this outfit of yours and I been waitin' my chance to hook up with you. Balmy, down at the Bit House, will okay me—so will China Sam and Pete Logan. Lots of these men of yours seen me before and know who I am."

He pointed to several familiar faces among the thieves, and was relieved when he saw them nod their heads in confirmation.

"You c'n use me, chief," he urged. "Maybe I don't look it, but when it comes to crackin' a crib I c'n hold my own with anybody in the racket. Don't need no soup, neither—just these," he rubbed his finger-tips together and warmed them with his breath.

"A safe-cracker, eh?" The voice sounded as if it were issuing from a hollow log, but Wentworth could detect the new interest in it—even thought that he saw the mask nod approval. "If you are as good as you say you are, perhaps I can use you. But first I'll give you a little test. Bring him this way."

With the black-robed leader, that thieves' procession marched downstairs and then to an empty room at one side of the loading-platform—a room which the masked individual unlocked with a key he took from beneath his robe. Switching on the unshaded electric bulb that illuminated it, he stood aside while Blinky was led in—waited until Solly Green was on hand, and then closed the door.

Against one wall of the room stood a large black safe. Blinky regarded it critically and then stooped to inspect it more closely. But suddenly he was thrust aside, and Solly Green stood peering at the time-worn black front. With a smothered oath, he whirled on the masked face.

"What in hell's the idea—" he began, but before he could get any farther the black-gowned leader waved his hand and a dozen of the thugs pounced on him and held him powerless.

"There is your test, Blinky," came from behind the mask. "Let me see how good you are—how long it will take you to solve that combination."

Some sort of tense drama hung in the air. Wentworth could sense that, but what it was he had no way of telling. Professionally, he spun the safe's dual dials—and gave silent thanks for the long hours spent under the tutelage of expert cracksmen. The eyes behind that mask were watching him like a hawk, and the thieves who hemmed him in on every side stared, fascinated, at this exhibition of a specialty to which only post-graduates in the crime school ever aspired.

To fail now would be to prove himself a fraud—to be exposed as an impostor and even identified as Richard Wentworth. That would mean death, swift and certain.

The backs of his hands were moist, as he knelt beside the massive safe, pressed his cheek against it and listened with super-sharp ears. But his fingers were steady. Surely, expertly, he turned the dials, catching the slightest click as the tumblers responded.

Not a sound broke the silence. Then came the almost inaudible grinding of the dials—a throaty gasp, an exclamation that was almost a moan, as the tumblers clicked into place. The outburst came from Solly Green, and the men holding him tightened their grip on his arms.

Blinky grasped the handles, pulled the doors wide. When he had unlatched the inner panels, he turned to the mask that loomed above him.

"Cinch," he grunted. "Any amateur coulda cracked an ancient crib like that. I thought you had something worth while."

"Very good, Blinky." The mask nodded, and the hollow voice seemed almost to purr. "This safe may not have been a very worthy test of your ability, but I am more than interested to see what it contains."

As he spoke, he bent over the pigeon-holes and pawed through their contents, discarding papers and notebooks until he found what he evidently was seeking—a leather-bound folio with notations that made his eyes gleam balefully through the slits in the mask.

"You have them all here, haven't you, Solly?" Now there was no mistaking the malice in his voice. "A complete roster of all who serve me. Fortunately, I heard that Kirkpatrick expected to secure a list of this sort. I knew that somebody must be planning to betray me—to sell out his comrades to the police. That's why I had this safe taken from your office and brought here, Solly—so that you could see for yourself what it contains, and explain it to us."

Solly Green had been planning to squeal to the commissioner! *That* was why Kirkpatrick had been so incensed at the thought of the Greens—Manny or Solly—leading this lawless outburst. *That* accounted for the air of bafflement, of mystification, Wentworth had sensed about the commissioner. Kirkpatrick must have believed he was being double-crossed....

"It's a frame!" Solly Green howled desperately. "You had my safe carted down here and got somebody to open it! You planted that stuff on me! Damn you, you can't get away with it, Dan!"

Out from beneath a slit in the robe now slid the blue-black muzzle of an automatic, gripped in a black-gloved hand. It was hardly visible against its ebon background—until orange flame spouted from its snout, and the closed room rang with the echoes of two shots that came almost as one. The frantic words died on Solly's lips, as a ghastly hole suddenly spouted in the center of his forehead. Blood was gushing from his chest even before his body slapped to the floor.

"That is the fate I mete out to traitors!" boomed the horrible mask as the gleaming eyes swiveled around the room, leaving a trail of shivery terror in their wake. "You, Blinky—I can use you. Do as you are told, and I will find a place for you—after you have proven yourself."

THEY WERE still standing there gaping down at Solly Green's body, watching his blood pool on the floor and trickle in a little stream under the safe that had betrayed him, when their bizarrely clad master strode from the room. Even after he had gone, the terror he inspired gripped them, and they spoke in whispers. Hesitantly, they clustered there in little, mumbling groups until a husky gorilla of a messenger came and summoned them by twos and threes.

When it was Blinky's turn, he was blindfolded and led out to a car. Someone else climbed into the seat behind him, and they were under way, speeding out into the night. At first, he tried desperately to orient himself, but that was hopeless. The blindfold had been too effectively tied in place, and he could pick up no sounds that might indicate what part of the city they were leaving. That warehouse was as complete a mystery to him as if he did not know that it existed.

But the man in the black robe and fantastic mask—Wentworth was almost certain he had met the fellow before. That subconscious sixth sense, which so rarely led him astray, seemed striving to make the identification—but there was nothing definite, nothing which would lead him anywhere....

When the car drew up at a curbstone and the blindfold was removed from his eyes, Wentworth blinked and shuddered away from the light until he had his hooded spectacles in place. But at the first glance he saw he was on the East Side within a few blocks of Holian Alley.

"Guess you can find your way home from here alone," his driver-captor grinned. "I'll be back for you tomorrow afternoon—about three o'clock. The boss will have a job for you, so don't slip up. He's not a good gent to cross—you saw that tonight."

Even after the fellow was gone, Wentworth had the queer feeling that he was being watched—that the gleaming eyes, behind that horrible mask, were able to follow his every movement.

Instead of going straight to his dingy room, he walked several blocks to a telephone and tried to reach Nita. But she was not at her hotel and had left no word for him at his home. Although she was well able to take care of herself, he was made uneasy. He didn't know her whereabouts, and a devil, such as this masked black-robe had threatened her....

Memory of those addle-brained policemen flashed into his mind; Barry Winant staggering brainlessly out of the freight elevator; Olga the maid, wandering around with a foolish grin on her face, meaningless words dribbling from her lips. In less than an hour, that cold-blooded fiend could murder Nita's brain and turn her into a demented creature! That thought sent a chill through Wentworth, while he shuffled back to Holian Alley.

Long after he sat down in the darkness of that dingy chamber, he mulled over what he had seen, trying to make a start toward solving the mystery which baffled him and, the entire police force of the city. Bit by bit, he went over all he had learned, reliving each adventure of the night. Again the identity of that masked leader seemed to tug at his memory, and he mentally recreated that scene with Solly.

Before he was shot down, Solly had started to call the masked man a name that sounded like Dan. Dan suggested Daniel Daley, one of the city's most influential gangster-politicians. It was Daley, Wentworth recalled, whom Barry Winant had accused of being Manny Green's higher-up and protector....

Could Daley be the masked leader? Or was it Victor Hanson,

the publisher—whom Wentworth had viewed with half-suspicion from the moment he appeared so opportunely at the scene of Thornton Sprague's death? Or, again, might it be Harvey Newell—whose ambition to fill Kirkpatrick's shoes was well known? Newell's zealous activity there at the Parker-Holland had been more than suspicious. He actually had seemed to enjoy the situation, taking obvious delight in pointing out its worst aspects to the newspapermen....

As he sat debating his problem, Wentworth was keeping watch on Catherine O'Keefe's lighted window next door. Twice he had leaped close to the window when there was the sound of footsteps, but it was only Catherine pacing the floor, restlessly—worrying, no doubt, about Ed Emmet.

Emmet was another unknown quantity in this criminal equation. Wentworth would have given a lot to know what became of him after the vans arrived at the warehouse. From that moment, he had dropped out of sight. Perhaps, like Solly Green, he had been disposed of for all time....

THE SOUND of Catherine O'Keefe's door opening put an end to Wentworth's speculation—and it was then that one question, at least, was answered. Ed Emmet was not dead. He was there in the room across the court, holding the girl in his arms as she sobbed out her relief.

"I've only a minute, Cath," he was saying. "I didn't want you to worry about me—and there's something I want you to do. Don't go to Lacy's tomorrow. Take a day off—never mind why. I can't tell you that, but I want you to do what I tell you. Keep away from the store tomorrow, no matter what you do. You'll understand by tomorrow night. Trust me that long, and you'll see that I know what I'm talking about."

There was more—soft-spoken, lovers' conversation so low that Wentworth could not catch it. However, again, as Emmet edged his way to the door, he exacted that curious promise.

Hoping to learn more of its significance, Wentworth slipped out of his room and downstairs as soon as the youth left. Close at his heels, he followed Emmet to the corner, saw him turn into the avenue and start toward a bus line. Wentworth hesitated there a moment, afraid to follow too closely for fear his quarry might turn and recognize him on the more brightly lit avenue. It would be better to let him get a bit farther ahead....

Emmet was now passing a taxi, parked at the curb. Buried in his thoughts, he paid no attention to it—when suddenly its door flew open and two men leaped out. Grabbing him, they literally pitched him into the cab. Instantly, they sprang in behind him, and the taxi started down the avenue.

All that had taken no more than a couple of seconds. Almost before Wentworth realized what had happened, the machine was speeding away. Hopelessly, he sprinted after it, knowing that he could not hope to overtake them. There was not another cab in sight.

Doggedly, he kept after it—muttered grim thanks when the corner traffic light turned red. Even that break did not promise much. The driver, stepping on the gas, was going to jump the light. Then, just as he reached the corner, he had to jam on his brakes—another cab had darted out of the side street.

That near-collision seemed to rattle the driver. He was slow on the take-off—and, before he got under way again, Wentworth was clinging to the rear spare tire. Carefully, he pulled himself up onto the roof so that he would not be seen passing the rear window. He worked cautiously up to the edge of the glass observation top—and immediately identified one of Emmet's captors. *Joe Tobin!*

"You're another wise-guy, ain't you?" the killer was sneering. "Thought you'd slip down here and spill your guts to your moll, didn't you? Never thought that little Joey might be trailing you, did you? That's where you wasn't so smart, see? You're going to get yours right here in this cab. Then we'll take care of your gal friend before she can do any yappin'."

"She doesn't know a thing," Ed pleaded with them. "I didn't tell her anything—I swear to God! You can't bring her into this—"

Tobin's chuckle was beastly, maddening. It made Emmet scuffle desperately to break loose.

"Grab his arms, Sam," Tobin ordered, as his fists beat against the captive's head, "Hold the dirty rat still. I want him to know how it feels to get six inches of steel in his belly."

With sadistic relish, he drew his knife and held it up so that the passing lights flashed on its blade. Then suddenly the top of the cab flew open and a black shape catapulted in on top of them!

Tobin screamed in agony, as his own knife plunged deep into his groin. Desperately, he tried to draw it out, but the automatic barrel that smashed down on his skull dropped him in a heap on the floor.

For the next thirty seconds, the interior of that cab was a madhouse. Penned in the narrow quarters, Wentworth dodged the murderous blow the thug, Sam, aimed and locked arms with him. Together, they heaved and tumbled, slamming against the sides, against the doors, crashing against the front windows where the terrified driver crouched over his wheel and jammed his foot on the brakes.

The moment the machine came to a stop, the driver leaped out and ran as if all the fiends of hell were pursuing him. The door flew wide, and Ed Emmet tumbled out onto the street. Without a backward glance, Emmet picked himself up and took flight in the opposite direction.

With his knees in the thug's belly, Wentworth got his fingers around the other's throat—steel fingers that tightened inexorably. He squeezed until the thug's eyes popped out of his head, tongue gagged out of his mouth, death-rattle gurgled.

As the limp body sagged back onto the seat, Wentworth glanced up and down the avenue. Nobody was near at hand, but, a block away, he thought he glimpsed the cab driver edging his way back cautiously toward the deserted machine.

Grimly, Wentworth reached into his pocket, and, when his fingers came out again, they grasped a thin silver cigarette lighter. But, instead of sparking its flame into life, he pressed the bottom of the gadget firmly against the center of Joe Tobin's forehead. Then he applied it in similar fashion to Sam's sweat-matted brow.

In both spots, that lighter left its mark—the indelible impression of a crimson spider. It was a warning to the slinking denizens of the underworld, and the unholy monster organizing them for war upon the city, that the Spider was once more to be reckoned with. When the scared driver mustered sufficient courage to come back to the cab, the sight that would greet him would send him scurrying off to his master. And the black-robed masquerader would realize at last that he was engaged in a battle from which only he or the Spider could emerge alive!

Blinky McQuade's eyes glinted behind his glasses, as he stepped out of the cab and closed the door behind him. For a moment, he hesitated, then darted into the shadows, slouching off into the night.

CHAPTER 6
CLOSING TIME FOR CORPSES

A S COMMISSIONER KIRKPATRICK had feared, next morning's papers were filled with scare-head crime news. The Central Park outrages, the Golden Palace horror, the murder of Dr. Sprague, the Parker-Holland hold-up, the armory raid—one piled on top of the other to confront the dismayed city with the most lawless night it ever had experienced. Crowning all these, was the terrible doom that had been inflicted upon Special Prosecutor Barry Winant—fearsome warning of what any prosecutor, police official or private citizen might expect who attempted to stem the rising tidal wave of crime.

That night, Wentworth had slept in Blinky McQuade's room—keeping awake until the sky grayed to be certain no attempt was made to molest Catherine O'Keefe. By the time he awoke, and shuffled out onto the street, Victor Hanson's *Evening Standard* was already on the stands with a special crime extra.

"The Mask of Madness Threatens New York!" it shouted, and the name thus bestowed on the criminal organizer sped from lip to lip—a terrifying sobriquet the metropolis would remember for many a year!

Out of Wentworth's thinking had come the decision to have a talk with Dan Daley. It would take a man of Daley's political power to ferret his way so deeply into the police department—such a power to overawe and fascinate the imagination of the criminal element, and organize a criminal campaign so daringly and devilishly effective.

From his squalid Holian Alley quarters, Blinky McQuade made his way east, toward the river. He reached a large, empty factory, the alley which ran beside it, and then one of a row of galvanized iron garages at its rear. When the door of that garage opened again, it was Richard Wentworth, immaculate as his Park Avenue friends knew him, who stepped out.

Twenty minutes later, Daniel Daley's heavy-featured face beamed when he recognized his visitor.

"Come in, Mr. Wentworth—come in!" he greeted heartily, as the doorman at his political clubhouse showed Wentworth into the reception-room. "Come back here where you can be comfortable."

When his caller was seated in an easy chair beside the huge, old fashioned roll-top desk, Daley leaned back in his swivel-chair and meditatively chewed on the butt of the cigar that never seemed to leave the corner of his mouth. His shrewd eyes studied this socialite who had made something of a reputation as a dilettante criminologist.

"Bet I know what's on your mind," he offered. "It's this hell that broke loose last night. Yeah, I thought so," as Wentworth made no denial. "It's the damnedest thing in my whole experience—and I've seen some raw jobs pulled. We've got to get together and put a stop to this—"

"What do you know about Solly Green, Daley?" Wentworth

Triumphantly, they drove back the masked
gunmen who were looting the store!

interrupted disconcertingly. "He wasn't killed for no reason. There was a purpose in wiping him out. Revenge—or to stop him from chiseling in on someone else's racket? Perhaps he knew too much, or because he intended to squeal—"

His eyes watched Daley's face with the intensity of a hawk, but the politician did not bat an eye. His cigar rolled from one side of his mouth to the other. He nodded again.

"I see what you're driving at, Mr. Wentworth," he admitted. "You believe that stuff Barry Winant's been spouting about me. You think I've been covering up for the Greens. Well, you're wrong. Manny used to come to me for favors, just like anyone else—but I hardly knew Solly. I haven't any idea why they wiped him out. From what I hear, I guess it's no great loss. I don't know who wiped him out," he insisted earnestly, "but I want to help round up his killer—just the same as I'd have helped nab him if he killed anyone else." He frowned.

"We can't sit back and tolerate conditions like this in our city," he waxed eloquent. "Nothing is safe—our streets, parks, homes. Such a situation is a national disgrace, and we've got to do something about it. I'm mighty glad you came this morning, Mr. Wentworth. We've got a committee meeting here in a few minutes that I know you'll be glad to join. We're going to call on Commissioner Kirkpatrick and demand better police protection. They're men outstanding in our municipal life—Colonel John Morgan, Bishop Callahan, Stephen Pomeroy, Aaron Fairchild, Roscoe Lonsdahl—people you know well. They asked me to organize them and get a hearing from the commissioner."

THE COMMITTEE that gathered in Daley's outer office

was all that he had claimed for it—a deputation of the city's most influential citizens. Conspicuous among them was dignified Aaron Fairchild and several of his Fifth Avenue neighbors, particularly incensed over the Central Park outrages committed almost in their dooryards.

"It isn't only last night's terrible incidents, you know," Fairchild protested, running nervous fingers through thin, graying hair. "Women have been molested and have actually disappeared in Central Park on several occasions during the past few weeks. It is getting so that the Avenue is no longer a safe place to walk, much less on which to make one's home."

That was the tenor of their complaint, when they were ushered into the police commissioner's office—the scandalous condition existing so close to their homes. Unless checked at once, real estate values would drop and the better element forced to leave the city for security.

Wentworth watched keenly, as they stated their case. Kirkpatrick's face was gray, eyes tired. He listened patiently and assured them that their homes would be safe. The police around the park would be doubled. One by one, Wentworth studied the committee members, but found nothing unusual about them—nothing unusual about anyone except Dan Daley.

As he studied the politician, he sensed that there was something familiar about his stride, the very way he carried himself—something strangely reminiscent of the Mask of Madness! Once that idea flashed into Wentworth's mind, it quickly took hold. Daley's unconscious mannerisms, he soon convinced himself, were those of the masked killer who had shot down Solly Green!

Unobtrusively, Wentworth edged his way to the door and took the first opportunity to slip out of the office while Kirkpatrick was still surrounded by the indignant committeemen. If Daley really was the Mask of Madness, there might be incriminating evidence in his office. While he was at headquarters, was the time to investigate his sanctum.

FROM HEADQUARTERS, Wentworth took a cab to a certain Bowery costumer who prided himself on being able to furnish any outfit at a moment's notice. Wentworth wanted to pass as a telephone-repair man—and, fifteen minutes later, when he rang the bell of Daley's district clubhouse, the doorman readily admitted the overall-clad workman whose arrival had been announced by phone ten minutes earlier.

The doorman stood by curiously while the supposed repair man took the telephone instrument apart, then lost interest and returned to the front of the building. While he worked, Wentworth's eyes had been inventorying Daley's office. The moment the doorman left, he went into action. In the center of the politician's desk were several latest editions of the afternoon papers, partially covering a sheaf of correspondence which projected from beneath.

Wentworth lifted the newspapers—and then stared down at another of those grim warnings that were becoming so familiar! Like the others, it was typewritten, signed only with a leering mad-head at the foot of its ominous message—

WARNING
Don't be a fool! Mind your own business! Your interference

will not be tolerated—and, if you persist, you are slated for a dose of the same medicine Barry Winant received. Only fools meddle with—

The Mask of Madness! Seemingly the cunning devil was able to plant those grisly threats wherever he chose....

Carefully, Wentworth replaced the newspapers as they had been, then made a hurried search of the rest of the desk. It revealed nothing incriminating or even suspicious. The only item of slight significance was a telephone memorandum that Victor Hanson had called and wanted Daley to phone him when he returned.

Victor Hanson... But there were innumerable reasons why the publisher should want to get in touch with a politician as potent as Daley—so that meant very little.

The sound of Daley's voice at the door snapped Wentworth into action. The telephone was already put together again, but he had no desire to test out his disguise under the politician's sharp scrutiny, or to be on hand when Daley discovered that threatening note. Grabbing his bag of tools, he hurried out of the office and down a rear stairs to the basement floor. From there, an entrance opened onto the backyard, which was separated only by a low fence from the property on the next street—an easy hurdle for a telephone-repair man prowling around in search of wire trouble.

As he made his way back to the Bowery costumer, he decided Dan Daley was no more a suspect than Stanley Kirkpatrick or Barry Winant. All three had received the same warning, threatened with the same fate. Yet his suspicion of the politician would not entirely down. That haunting similarity of mannerisms, gestures....

Perhaps it was all in his own imagination, Wentworth rebuked himself. Once the idea had sprouted in his mind, he had fed it, bolstered it up in his eagerness to find a tangible clue. Shortly, he hoped, he would have another opportunity to study the black-robed masquerader. Meanwhile, he might be able to pick up some worthwhile information in the resorts from which many of the Mask's men had been recruited.

THINGS WERE unusually quiet in the congested tenement district, Blinky McQuade noticed, as he made his way from one rendezvous to the other. Familiar faces were absent to such a degree that the district seemed half-stripped of its population. Bars usually crowded were now practically empty—patronized only by shabby down-and-outers of no use to anybody.

Even Balmy's Bit House had apparently been hit by the change. When Blinky had passed the guard at the door, and been admitted to the inner holy of holies where none but penitentiary graduates were allowed to set foot, he was surprised to find the place deserted. The bar, where standing room usually was at a premium, was empty—only a few customers lounged at the tables.

"Business ain't so hot," Blinky observed when the broken-nosed, cauliflower-eared proprietor ranged up beside him at the bar.

But Balmy wasn't worried. He winked knowingly, and a grin spread over his ring-battered features.

"Not so good today maybe," he admitted, "but there's good

times coming—very soon. But I'll bet you know more about that than I do." He chuckled, as he sauntered back to his office in the rear.

Wentworth sensed that air of expectancy, eager anticipation. The underworld was like a secret revolutionary army, lying low, waiting only for the call to rise and take over. The word from the Mask of Madness, would turn them loose on the helpless city like a pack of ravening wolves. That word must never be allowed to come!

By three o'clock, Blinky was back in Holian Alley waiting for his conductor from the Mask. But it was nearly four before the sardonic-faced thug arrived and announced that the car awaited. This time there was no blindfold. Yet the driver kept a close mouth and ignored Blinky's attempts to draw him into conversation.

Their destination was the back room of an old-time saloon on Eighth Avenue—a large room crowded with men when they arrived. Despite the seeming lack of organization or discipline in that milling, drinking crowd, Wentworth noticed that each knew his leader, what was expected of him. One by one, groups congregated and then left, until not more than a dozen remained in the room.

"Our turn now," his guide warned. "The rest have gone ahead to clear the way. All we'll have to do is walk in, help ourselves. In case you didn't know it—we're going shopping in Lacy's."

Lacy's huge department store! The regiment of thieves was to be turned loose in it—to sack it from top to bottom! That was why Ed Emmet had begged Catherine O'Keefe not to go to work today. He had known of this impending coup—and kept the knowledge to himself!

If only Wentworth could slip away from his thug companions, there might still be time to get in touch with Kirkpatrick… But his captor's sardonic grin mocked him.

The thugs, Wentworth noticed, hemmed him in on all sides, watching him alertly, as they marched toward the great shopping center. The man at his side was menacing; Wentworth felt the fingers on his elbows, the muzzle of the automatic pressed against his ribs.

"Just so that you don't get any nutty ideas and make us kill a lot of people here on the street," the gunman muttered.

By the clock in a store window, Wentworth saw that it was almost five-thirty as they filed through Lacy's main entrance. Store employees were already stationed at the doors, waiting the signal to close them and bar farther customers. Five-thirty— the doors closed, the shades were lowered, and at that moment the largest department store in New York City passed into the hands of the Mask of Madness!

ONE MOMENT, everything seemed to be as usual; the next, a swarm of men, wearing leering-faced masks that covered their heads, seemed to be everywhere. With machine-like precision, they converged on their objectives. Wentworth saw them closing in on the main entrance. Blackjacks and gun-barrels thudded down on the skulls of the doormen. The doors were locked and the hideous-masked guards backed up against them, automatic muzzles trained on the terrified customers begging to be let out.

While those devils saw to it that no victim escaped, that no possible word of what was occurring behind the drawn blinds seeped out to the crowded street outside, their mates ranged up and down the aisles by the dozens. Looting and smashing, they went from counter to counter, grabbing anything that seized their fancy. Then they turned on the helpless customers, snatching their purses, stripping them of their valuables, manhandling any who dared resist.

The shrieks of terrified women rang in Wentworth's ears. His blood boiled as he saw those wretched devils pawing women, submitting them to every indignity. Gun barrels whipped down into innocent faces, the weapons red with blood. Men and women were lying in the aisles, kicked out of the way as the masked horde swarmed over them!

"They'll take care of things down here, all right," his companion snapped. "They won't need us—and there's better pickings upstairs. That's where you come in, Blinky—in case they manage to close the safes before the boys can take over."

Docilely, Blinky shuffled along, apparently awed, and anxious only to save his own skin. With his special guard on one side, another thug on the other, he stepped into an elevator. He huddled in the back of the car while the hoodlums bullied the cowering operator. Almost wild with fear, the mulatto stood trembling at his controls, eyes milky pools of terror as he glanced at the automatic muzzles menacing him.

Too anxious to please, the operator braked the car ahead of time, then overshot the floor as he tried to rectify his mistake.

"Clumsy baboon!" the weazen-faced gunman who stood

beside him snarled—and whipped at his head with a pistol barrel.

With a groan, the panic-stricken operator relinquished the control, staggered back against a side wall of the car. But, just before his hand dropped clear, he had started the car upward. Now it continued up the shaft, unguided—until the thug beside Wentworth made a leap for the control.

That was the opportunity for which Wentworth had been praying. Instantly, he took advantage of it. Bristling into unexpected action, he whipped his right fist up under the jaw of the fellow who had gun-whipped the operator, then hurled himself upon the back of the other thug. Before that startled individual knew what had happened, Wentworth's left arm closed around his throat, held the automatic and tried to wrest it loose.

The thug was stronger than Wentworth expected. He fought back so stubbornly that Wentworth could not seize the weapon. The other man leaped at him, face twisted into a savage snarl, gun raised for the knockout smash. Desperately, Wentworth thrust one leg between those of the men he held, twisted it around and put all his strength into a *jiu-jitsu* hold that flipped both to the floor of the car—dumped them in a heap.

"Gawd A'mighty!" the terrified operator gasped, as he shuddered away from the wildly flailing fists and crazily twisting, squirming bodies.

Wentworth was grabbed by the collar, half dragged to his feet and slammed back against the wall of the car. But, as he hit the floor, his hand closed on the weapon his guard had dropped. In the next instant, he bounded back like a rubber ball, smashing the heavy barrel into the face of first one cursing thug, then the other. Just in time, he pulled the trigger and flung himself out of the way—as the second thug fired.

The double explosion in that tiny, metal-walled car was like sledge-hammers beating on an empty boiler. Stunned as much by the terrific noise, as by the blow on the back of his head, he threw himself against the side of the car to dodge that bullet. Wentworth stared at one dead man, and another whose face was covered with blood as he tried to get to his knees. That man tried to pick up the pistol that had fallen from his hand, got his fingers on it—

Deliberately, Wentworth shot him through the head, as he would have executed a mad dog. Then he turned to the trembling operator, who was begging for mercy, fully expecting that the next shot was intended for him.

"The sporting goods department—get me there in a hurry," Wentworth snapped, and the whiplash tone of his voice had its effect.

The shaking operator stepped squeamishly over the dead bodies, and manned the controls; the car moved. The moment the door opened, Wentworth sprang out. This floor seemed almost deserted—which was exactly what he wanted. Diving behind a counter, he unbuttoned his vest and shirt and took from around his body a thin package which yielded a long black cloak and a floppy-brimmed black felt hat.

With a make-up kit, which came from inside the lining of his coat, he went to work on his face. Like magic, the features, that were Blinky McQuade's, disappeared. Into their place came the vulpine visage that was a terror to the bravest of the underworld habitues. It was an incredibly ugly face, with shaggy eyebrows and snaggly teeth set in a mouth that seemed lipless—a demoniacal face framed with lanky strands of matted black hair and crowned by that flopping travesty of a hat.

CREEPING, CROUCHING, like the creature from which he took his name, the Spider made his way to the section of the floor on which the sporting goods were located. As he expected, half a dozen of the masked thieves were in control there.

With a cackling laugh that chilled men's souls, the Spider suddenly leaped into view behind a counter, guns thundering as fast as he could pull the triggers. Those guns of retribution cut thieves down where they stood—caught the last squealing thug who tried desperately to scuttle to safety.

"The Spider!" one of the amazed clerks gasped incredulously.

"Yes—the Spider!" Wentworth rasped in a harsh, discordant voice. "The Spider—looking for *men!* You fellows are the one hope of saving this store from the hands of thieves who will loot and burn it to the ground. If there are any real men among you, follow me! Arm yourselves with those rifles and pistols. Take as many as you can carry for your fellow employees, and as much ammunition as you can manage. Follow me—and in ten minutes we'll have rounded up every criminal rat in the building!"

His leadership was magnetic. Eagerly, the clerks rallied to it. Using the sporting goods department as an arsenal, he recruited his band and led the way to the elevators. One by one, they seized the cars from the surprised thugs who guarded them.

Then, four carloads full at one time, they started down to the ground floor.

In a flying wedge, with the Spider at its apex, they surged out onto the street floor and into a scene of the wildest panic.

"Down on the floor, you customers!" Wentworth shouted. With flaming guns, his clerk army swept forward, trading shot for shot with the surprised and disconcerted thugs.

Triumphantly, they drove the masked gunmen before them, cleared a way to the main entrance and the street—when suddenly a terrific explosion rocked the store. After it came another… and another. With the concussions came sheets of flame, clouds of gas—gas that settled over the counters like a stifling blanket!

Fighting desperately to keep his head clear, to find some spot where that strangling gas had not already penetrated, Wentworth staggered across the store. He reached the up-going escalator and stumbled onto it, clinging to the leather belt with his fingers. Dimly, he could see that chaotic hell beneath him—a sea of struggling, screaming humans, with upturned, agonized faces.

The gas was filling his eyes with tears, blinding him, but he forced his smarting lids apart. He *had* to keep them apart, for he had seen—*yes, he had seen Nita!* There she was in the midst of that wild riot, fighting to get to him—holding her arms out to him imploringly!

Wentworth dragged himself to his feet, tried to start back down the moving escalator. Then his knees buckled, his legs gave way beneath him, and he felt himself falling… falling through a sea of roaring blackness that completely inundated him….

CHAPTER 7
THE SHADOW OF THE MASK

WHEN NITA VAN SLOAN had seen Wentworth follow the police cordon into Central Park, the impulse to follow him proved almost irresistible. She had long since learned to steel herself to these terrifying dangers which seemed to be his lot in life. She had reconciled herself to being companion and helper to this man whom she loved more than life itself.

But to watch him walking into peril alone was more than she could bear. She wanted to be near him, to share his hazards.

At a distance she followed him, watched him trailing the police as they searched every clump of shrubbery, every nook and corner. Then she had seen him spring to the aid of a girl and her companion who leaped from a covert in the bushes. When Richard Wentworth raised his hand against a policeman, there must be ample reason for it—and she knew at once that he wanted these young people to reach safety.

They were running right toward her, and Nita waved them on. She waited for them, and took the girl by the arm as if they had been old friends.

"Talk to me," she said in a conversational tone. "Act as if we are well acquainted. Some of these policemen know me and won't question you, if they think you are my friends."

Without interference, she led the way out of the park and to the sedan, held the rear door open for them. Then she took her place at the wheel.

"Better sit on the floor," she advised, as the car got under way.

"I'm quite sure I can get through alone, but they might want to question a man."

Nobody attempted to stop her, as she drove past the police cars drawn up around the park. Once out of the danger zone, onto a side street, she breathed a sigh of relief. Then she stiffened, as the cold muzzle of a pistol pressed against the back of her neck.

"Draw up to the curb and stop," the youth in the back seat said against her ear; and then, when she had complied, "That's right. Now get out and come back here. Don't try to run when you step into the street—I don't want to shoot, unless I have to."

There was something in his tense voice—something in the desperate look in the eyes of the girl—that made Nita believe they meant just what he said. Helplessly, she obeyed orders. She climbed into the rear and sat there while they gagged and tied her up. Stretched out on the back seat, she watched the lights whizzing by as the car sped northward, until finally it was parked on a quiet, little frequented block.

And there they left her—to fight with the rope they had lashed around her wrists and ankles. The frightened look in that girl's face—the grim set of the young fellow's jaw—baffled her as much as the unusual way in which her assistance had been rewarded.

Still wondering about the inexplicable experience, she finally got home to her apartment—only to find her maid wandering about in a mental fog, eyes vacant, jaw hanging loose. Nita shook her, shouted at her, tried to slap her back to normality. But the girl was lost. Nothing could remove that insane grin from her face or stop the unintelligible babble drooling from her lips.

With a lump in her throat, tears in her eyes, Nita watched a hospital interne lead the girl away. "Hopelessly insane," he had whispered his verdict. Only a few hours before Olga had been a perfectly normal, light-hearted girl....

Thoughtfully, Nita stared at the maniacal soap face that grinned at her from the middle of her mantel-clock. That horrible thing was a warning that Olga's fate hung over her, too. It had been stuck there during the past few hours—possibly put in place while she lay helplessly tied up in the back of the sedan.

It didn't make sense. If that youth and his girl were mixed up with the criminal who used that leering face as a talisman, why had Dick helped them to avoid arrest? And, if they were not part of the criminal gang—if they did not want to keep here away from her apartment until this deviltry could be completed— what other reason could they have had for kidnaping her and leaving her tied up for hours?

NITA HAD already packed a light bag to leave the apartment and check in at the Raleigh, as Wentworth had directed, but on the way out she stopped at the parked sedan and searched it thoroughly. Carefully, she played a tiny flashlight into every corner of the rear seat—until it glinted on a bit of metal almost buried between the cushion and the side of the car. It proved to be an oval tag barely more than an inch long, stamped with the number *15492* and the name *Lacy's*.

Nita recognized it immediately. It was an employee's identification tag from Lacy's department store—something to be investigated in the morning.

Leaving the car for Jackson, Wentworth's chauffeur, to pick up, Nita taxied to the Raleigh and checked in under the alias she used in similar emergencies. Once in her rooms, the tragic events that started the evening came back into her thoughts. Alicia Sprague's mystifying disappearance made her afternoon telephone conversation even more puzzling and significant. Now Nita knew that there had been adequate cause for her friend's anxiety.

Alicia must have known what was going to happen, hoping against hope that Dick might be able to forestall it. Undoubtedly, it was why she had been so anxious to have him come with Nita that evening. Perhaps Alicia had been able to leave some message there in the house which the police had overlooked. There might be some clue to indicate what had happened to Alicia—a clue which only the eyes of a woman might detect.

Nita decided to investigate, anyway.

With the aid of the Sprague housekeeper, who had returned from a motion-picture performance to discover the tragedy that had occurred during her absence, Nita got by the police guard at the door and gained admittance to the house. Together, they searched Alicia's rooms. Everything seemed to be in order except, perhaps, envelopes addressed to Alicia from a private sanitarium in the city. It was a sanitarium noted for mental cases.

Into Nita's mind flashed a memory of that maniacal face leering at her from the dial of her clock—the horrifying soap cast

Dr. Sprague had clutched in his dead hand... and she slipped one of those envelopes into her pocket.

It was late, but her hunch was so impelling that she decided to go at once to the sanitarium. Most of the regular staff were off duty when she arrived, but a night clerk readily remembered Alicia Sprague having been there.

"Let me see," he mused. "She came to visit Scott Crawford. He was a brilliant young scientist attached to the Columbia University faculty until he became ill. Miss Sprague was greatly concerned about him."

From a filing cabinet, the clerk took a folder, leafed through it until he found Scott Crawford's record.

"Crawford was under treatment here until about a month ago," he reported. "At that time, he was removed to be taken to a convalescent home—we have no record of which one. He was signed out by authority of the university's board of trustees."

Scott Crawford... The name was familiar. Then Nita placed it. She remembered meeting him at a reception at the Sprague's, recalling his attentiveness to Alicia—and the girl's responsive-

NITA VAN SLOAN

ness. Yes, she remembered Crawford's thin, sharp-featured face and curiously penetrating eyes....

There was nothing further to be learned at the sanitarium. Nor was there anywhere else to inquire about him at that time of night. Perhaps in the morning she might be able to discover what had become of him—but in the morning there was something more important, more immediate, to occupy Nita's attention.

OUT OF bed early, she donned a plain, serviceable dress and

made herself up to counterpart a shopgirl. Before the store was open, she had found a place near the Lacy's employees' entrance from which she could watch the steady stream of workers come through the doorway. Intently, she eyed each girl who passed— until she spotted the one she had helped escape from Central Park.

So the girl did work in Lacy's! The next step, then, was to become acquainted with her, and win her confidence.

As soon as the store was opened to the public, Nita went in and began her search—a task which ended when she located the girl she sought behind a counter in the cosmetics department. In the center of that counter was a young woman demonstrating Nonpareil beauty preparations. Nita's problem was solved.

Alvin Holmes was the general manager of the Nonpareil Corporation, and Alvin never had learned how to say "no."

"All I want you to do is to give your demonstrator in Lacy's a holiday for the rest of the day and perhaps tomorrow," Nita explained, when she sat before his desk. "Let me take her place— and I'll show you how Nonpareil creams should be demonstrated! Please Alvin—it's extremely important that I do this or I wouldn't ask it."

Holmes seemed a little amazed by that proposition, but had no objection to having Nita van Sloan demonstrate his products. An hour later, the regular demonstrator was recalled to the office, and Nita stepped into her place and began the round of face-daubing and lecturing which would be hers for the rest of the day.

In the crisp blue-and-white Nonpareil smock, which covered

her dress, she had little fear of recognition from the Central Park girl—who had only seen her at night in the semi-darkness of the sedan. The girl's name, she soon learned, was Catherine O'Keefe; by noon, they had become well acquainted.

All day Nita watched her closely, but the girl paid attention to her job and nobody bothered her. Nobody, in any way suspicious, contacted her. Closing time approached, and Nita cleaned up her table and took off her smock so as to be ready to leave as promptly as the O'Keefe girl.

Five-thirty. The department began to close—when suddenly terrific screams rang out, and down the aisle swept a horde of fantastically masked men, driving the panic-stricken customers and clerks before them at the muzzles of automatics and sub-machine guns!

NITA'S EYES flashed to Catherine O'Keefe. The girl's face was ashen-white, her eyes wide pools of horror, as she huddled back against the shelves. One of the masked men saw her there and leaped over the counter to grab her. But, at that moment, another came running down the aisle and sprang between them. He whispered something in the girl's ear—and the last bit of color drained from her face as she backed away from him, aghast.

With a vile curse, the displaced raider whirled on the newcomer, lashing out at him with an automatic. The descending weapon crashed down on the maniacal mask, tore through the papier-mâché—and through the fantastic wreckage peered the face of Catherine O'Keefe's companion in the park!

Before he could recover from that stunning impact, the youth went down under a barrage of blows from half a dozen of his fellows. Nita and the girl were seized, then dragged off under the direction of another of the masked marauders who seemed to be giving orders.

Through the panic-stricken, wildly milling throng, they were rushed, gun muzzles jabbing in their ribs to discourage resistance. Nita tried desperately to free herself, but the burly brute who gripped her arm twisted it mercilessly and guffawed, as the tears ran down her cheeks. Hopelessly, she yielded, gave up the vain struggle, and allowed him to prod her onward.

All around them hell had broken loose. The hysterical screams of women mingled with the terrified yells of men, punctuated by the roar of guns and the crash of wrecked showcases—then were drowned by a succession of blasts that threatened to bring the whole building down on their heads. Terrific explosions brought flames in their wake; flames and clouds of gaseous smoke clutched at Nita's throat. But none of this seemed to have any effect on the masked devils.

Blindly, Nita staggered along—until suddenly a hideously ugly face seemed to loom in the smoke cloud ahead of her. The Spider! He was there on the escalator, being borne up to the floor above!

Nita screamed wildly. In sheer desperation, she managed to tear herself loose and stagger toward the Spider, arms held out to him. He saw her! He was on his feet—coming down to her!

But he swayed dizzily, then crumpled to the escalator steps—just as she was seized around the waist and dragged, half-unconscious, through the store to the shipping-room and then out to the loading platforms. Like a sack of produce, she was tossed into a truck that looked like a small van, left there beside Catherine O'Keefe, to struggle to her knees and creep into a corner of the dark interior.

That truck was a queer place. At one end was a box somewhat like a portable radio, placed on a low packing case. Near the doorway was a man, in the uniform of Lacy's special policemen, standing against the wall, his hands above his head fastened to the side of the truck with leather straps. He was giggling foolishly. When one of the masked men came in and released him, he staggered out onto the loading platform as if drunk....

Nita heard his crazy laughter ringing hollowly in her ears. It seemed to be fading, getting farther and farther away—and then it was gone entirely as the darkness closed in and lulled her senses to sleep.

CHAPTER 8
MACHINE-MADE MADNESS

WHEN THE Spider opened his eyes and gasped for breath, it was as if a great hand had been clapped over his face, smothering him while he rocked back and forth dizzily. For an instant, that suffocating grip was loosened—then he managed to fill his lungs with clean air.

Gradually, his swimming senses began to clear, objects around him becoming steady. The mist faded from before his eyes, and he could hear, think....

In a flash, his situation came back to him. He was lying at the head of the escalator on the second floor; the moving steps had rolled his body off to one side. Nobody was near him, but, down below on the street floor, bedlam was still raging. Men were shouting and cheering, women screaming in hysterical relief. The blue coats of policemen were worming through the press. They were at the foot of the escalator, on their way up, to complete the rout of the masked bandits still remaining in the building.

Only then did Wentworth realize his own position. The first policeman who saw him would pounce upon him or empty a pistol into his body. They would not know that the Spider had organized and led that little band of clerks to battle the thieves, long enough to break out of the store and summon help. But for the Spider the great retail establishment might have been burned to the ground with a loss of thousands of lives. Yet, if the police trapped him, he need expect no mercy.

Groggily, Wentworth staggered to his feet. He must get out of his Spider costume—must even rid himself of Blinky McQuade's shabby rags before the police grabbed him and held him as one of the raiders.

The men's clothing department—that was the answer! Wentworth stumbled across the floor to the stairway, drove himself up the steps. He breathed a sigh of relief when he saw that the clothing department was deserted except for two corpses who lay where they had fallen when the gunmen's bullets cut them down.

Quickly, he shed cape and hat; pulled off the black wig and went to work on his face with speeding fingers. From a clothes' dummy, he stripped a tweed suit that should be about his size. A shirt and tie from one of the showcases, a soft felt hat… and, in a surprisingly short time, every vestige of the Spider—every slovenly trace of Blinky McQuade—had vanished, and Richard Wentworth was stooping over one of the dead men, seemingly trying to revive him. Then the police came surging through the department.

"I managed to dive into one of the dressing rooms and save myself. These poor fellows weren't so lucky," he explained, when the officers reached them. "Have you rounded up that pack of murderers?"

"Nary a one," a grizzled sergeant spat in disgust. "Some dead ones down on the first floor and some more up in the sporting-goods department—but the rest slipped away slick as sin."

That was the truth. When the store had been searched from top to bottom the police had rounded up the corpses of fifteen dead thugs—fifteen well known crooks, killed by the Spider, or the clerks he organized, or murdered by their own companions so that, wounded, they would not fall alive into the hands of the police!

There were eight men who would have been better off dead—six of the special store-policemen, and two members of the regular department, who stood around and watched with grinning, vacuous faces from which all vestige of sanity had fled.

Those madmen had a profound effect on the police, Wentworth noticed the moment they appeared. Their brother officers looked at them with blanched, awe-stricken faces—edged away fearfully to stand muttering among themselves.

"Johnson," he heard one of the bluecoats say to another, "that's the tall, blond feller there—he got a warning last night. Someone called up and told him to take sick leave today if he knew what was good for him. He laughed at it—but now look at him!"

So the mask had reached the point where he actually was threatening the police, warning them to stay away when he wanted no interference! Kirkpatrick should know about that, Wentworth thought grimly—but Kirkpatrick did know about it.

"That's nothing new," the commissioner admitted, as soon as he arrived at the raided store and Wentworth was able to get his ear. "I've been hearing rumors of warnings of that sort all day—and these aren't the first men to suffer for not doing what the Mask ordered. Nine of my patrolmen have been stricken with madness since this morning. He has been striking all over town, deliberately scattering his attacks to demonstrate that he can hit where he pleases."

Grim-faced, Kirkpatrick looked at the latest victims of this frightful scourge. Wentworth could fairly see his soul writhing in torment. Before his very eyes, the commissioner was seeing his department demoralized and wrecked.

"I can't blame them," he murmured, as he read the stark fear in the eyes of his onlooking men. "Panic is spreading all through the department, Dick. My desk is loaded down with reports of insubordination, suspensions, resignations, cowardice, such as we've never known on the New York City force. But I can't blame them. My men are not afraid of death—you know that. But they are only human. They quail at this awful threat of madness that hangs over them constantly. This Mask of Madness, whoever he is, is out to get me. He is determined to drive me out of office—and I fear he is going to succeed. The storm is rising—"

As he spoke, Kirkpatrick took a copy of the *Evening Standard* from his topcoat pocket, unfolded it. Wentworth could see the heavy black headline demanding a reorganization, from the commissioner down, of the police department.

"Hanson is already demanding my resignation," he said bitterly. "He is boosting Harvey Newell for my post—but you know how poorly Newell is qualified for the job. He's a weakling, a spineless parader. He would be putty in the hands of the crooks or whoever is behind them. I would be willing to resign, if I knew that a worthwhile man would succeed me—but to get out for Harvey Newell would be to turn the city over to this Mask of Madness and his army of thieves!"

Kirkpatrick was going to stick on the job and fight—the dogged set of his jaw left no doubt of that. Yet he had no actual leads; nothing but his own half-formed suspicions. Wentworth *had* to have more than that. Nita was gone, in the hands of those crooks. The memory of that last of her, reaching out to him appealingly, stabbed him to the heart. She had appealed—and he had failed her!

Perhaps, at that very moment, that black-robed fiend who hid behind a maniacal mask was torturing, driving her into hopeless insanity!

That ghastly thought drove Wentworth berserk. He *had* to find her! But where? How could he even begin to track down the heartless murderer who laughed at the entire police force and struck down its members as he chose?

Only two suspects seemed to offer the slightest hope—Victor Hanson and Dan Daley. And Daley apparently was in as much danger as the rest of the city. That left only Hanson. It was a slim chance, but there were questions Wentworth wanted the publisher to answer. Undoubtedly, he would be in his office now, personally superintending the handling of the news on this latest criminal outrage.

WENTWORTH TAXIED downtown. Half expecting an excuse that Hanson was too busy to see him, he went up to the second-floor office—and obtained admission with surprising ease. Nobody was in the outer office. No one was there to stop him when he crossed between the empty desks and stepped up to the door of Hanson's private sanctum.

The lights were turned on in the inner office—but there was no answer when Wentworth knocked. Curiously, he turned the knob, opened the door on a crack. Hanson was sitting there at his big, flat-topped desk—a graven image, staring straight ahead of him with wide, horror-fixed eyes! Those eyes rested upon a metal box about the size of a portable radio, placed on the desk before him.

Even when Wentworth stepped through the doorway, the publisher did not bat an eye. Fixedly, he stared at that box, veins standing out on his forehead, beads of perspiration running down his face. Wentworth saw that he was strapped into his chair, arms pinioned so that he could not move—only sit there and stare as if he were looking into the face of death itself.

"What's the matter, Hanson?" Wentworth stepped forward. Now he saw that horror in the publisher's eyes was already tinged with madness, twisting into a foolish gleam. "What's happened to you, man?"

"Keep away," a surprising voice from behind the partially open door of Hanson's side closet answered those questions. "Stay right where you are—hands out where I can see them. Don't move—unless you want to drop where you stand."

The ugly snout of an automatic snaked out around the edge of the door to enforce those commands. But the man's face was hidden in the shadows of the closet.

Wentworth shrugged resignedly. "All right," he capitulated—but suddenly flung himself to one side, grabbed for the office door, shouted, "I'll get help!" as he bolted for it. He reversed himself, in a split-second.

The gun at the closet door roared. A bullet smashed through the glass of the office door. But just as the hidden man dived out of his ambush, Wentworth struck him—grabbed him around the knees in a flying tackle and bounced him down onto the floor. In a moment he had his man disarmed, gripped helplessly—and was looking down into the desperate face of Ed Emmet!

"Let me go!" the lad pleaded frantically. "You can't stop me now—just when I have that rat where I want him! He's part of this criminal gang—don't you understand? He and Dan Daley—they're in it together. I used to work for Daley. I was his secretary, until he fired me because I got wise. That's why he had my sister kidnaped," he groaned.

"Don't look at me that way!" he fairly yelled as he saw the doubt and suspicion in Wentworth's eyes. "I know what I'm talking about. Dan Daley is the Mask of Madness—I've seen him in his black robe and mask. I'd know him no matter how he tried to disguise himself. But I couldn't get at him. That's why I came here, to force a confession out of this rat who is working with him!" He was panting.

"The murdering devils—they have Catherine and Florence, my sister. That's why you saw me in Central Park last night. I was patrolling the park, trying to find out what those skunks did with my sister. Three nights ago, they grabbed her there—took her right away from the man she was with, just the way they did last night to those other girls. They've got a hideout there somewhere in the park—they must have! That's what I was looking for when all that trouble started."

"That's why you have been running around with the Mask's crooks ever since, eh?" Wentworth hurled at him. "That's why you shot down a lot of innocent people in the Golden Palace dance hall?"

Emmet's eyes bugged out with amazement.

"I didn't—" he began, and then gave that up as useless. "I saw Joe Tobin there in the park," he confessed. "I knew him. The minute I saw that he was tied up with that gang, I had him where I wanted him. I made him vouch for me, get me in with the gang. I wanted to get the goods on them and land them all in jail for what they did to my kid sister…" His voice was shaking.

Emmet's frantic explanations were becoming almost hysterical. Helplessly he stood by as, Wentworth bent over the metal box curiously, found the switch which operated it, and turned it off.

As soon as the current was turned off, a strange change came over Hanson's face. The tension relaxed, his eyes lost their utter horror. Gradually, the foolish grin disappeared. Slowly, he regained control of his faculties, and then his lips moved uncertainly at first, then more confidently.

"Lies—crazy lies!" he scoffed at Emmet's story. "I don't know a thing about the Mask. I was sitting here at my desk when this lunatic broke in and shoved a gun into my face. He strapped me to the chair and then started that infernal contraption going in front of me—started all hell popping and roaring inside my skull...."

He had reached across the desk and taken hold of the box, examining it, curiously. "Some sort of an electrical set," he muttered, as he switched it on again and listened. "Appears to be a vibrator of some sort—"

"You know what it is, all right!" Emmet fairly sobbed in his frustration. "It's one of the boxes you and the Mask use to drive people insane. I saw it working down at Lacy's—a special cop strapped up in front of it until he became a raving maniac. I managed to steal this out of the van in the confusion. I brought it down here to give you a taste of your own rotten medicine!"

Wentworth had found a way to open the top of the box, and now he saw that it was, as Hanson had surmised, an electrical vibrator—a devilishly constructed machine which produced a succession of current waves that would batter against a human brain until the brain cells were demoralized and completely destroyed. It was so ingeniously conceived that a helpless victim, tied up in front of it, would go hopelessly insane in a matter of minutes once it started to work upon him.

That was how policemen could be stricken while walking their beats! They were grabbed, taken into one of those van-like trucks, strapped up while one of these infernal machines was turned loose upon them—then, hopeless maniacs, they were turned loose again to wander about the streets.

Wentworth did not know which of these two men to believe. Young Emmet's tale was so bizarre that it sounded fantastic. Yet, his desperate sincerity was somehow convincing. Hanson, on the other hand, seemed to have forgotten his vindictiveness. Now he was all the newspaperman, examining that devilish mechanism with shining eyes. Before Wentworth could stop him, he had grabbed up his desk phone and called for a photographer.

"Emmet is going out of here with me," Wentworth decided suddenly. "You're not going to have him arrested, Hanson. I'm out to round up this Mask and his criminal horde. Emmet may be able to help me."

Hanson shrugged and again reached for his phone. "Get him out of here—that's all," he conditioned his agreement. "Just keep him away from me with his crazy notions."

AS HE walked out of the *Standard* office with Emmet, Wentworth's busy brain was working at top speed. If the youth's story was true, he could be used. His anxiety about his missing sister, and Catherine O'Keefe, might be turned to good advantage, in locating them—and Nita. Quickly, Wentworth fabricated a plan, instructing Emmet just what he was to do and how to report developments.

"This is your only hope of locating Catherine and your sister," he concluded. "Fighting with Hanson will get you nowhere— except in jail. If you start trouble with Daley, you will come off just as badly. Do as I tell you and we'll round up the whole mob—Daley and Hanson with them, if they do have a hand in this thing."

Wentworth didn't know what to think about Daley and Hanson. The case against the politician looked bad, as Emmet outlined it. But there seemed nothing definite against the publisher, except Ed Emmet's unsupported suspicions....

And then, half an hour after they had left the *Evening Standard* office, a special edition of the paper was on the streets.

Wentworth bought a copy of the extra and stared at the photograph that occupied the entire front page except for the headline that shouted, "The Machine that Drives Men Mad!" There it was—a full-page picture of the vibrator. The next two pages were filled with a harrowing account of its operation, a lurid story of the Lacy hold-up, and a terror-breeding resume of the crime wave to date.

That layout could have but one effect. It would fan the flames, add to the panic sweeping the city. As he stared at the offending extra with angry eyes, Wentworth wondered whether, after all, Victor Hanson was innocent. Had the publisher outwitted him and cleverly landed a paralyzing blow by thus broadcasting the menace which hung over all who disobeyed the commands of the ruthless Mask of Madness?

When he reached his Sutton Place home, Wentworth wondered again....

There, glued to the door of the apartment, which he used only as a blind and entrance to the stronghold on the edge of the river behind it, was a typewritten message. One of those leering soap faces was affixed to the message which he now read-

WARNING

Nita van Sloan, as you may have suspected, is my guest. How long she remains in that capacity depends upon you. Stop your interference, or she will take her place in the ranks of the brainless ones!

A devilish warning from the Mask of Madness. It had been pasted up there on the door less than an hour after Wentworth had declared, in Victor Hanson's presence, his intention of rounding up the master criminal....

CHAPTER 9
GAUNTLET OF DEFIANCE

B Y THE next morning, the Mask of Madness had thrown off all restraint. Hot on the heels of the sensation, caused by the *Evening Standard's* extra with its terror-breeding photograph and drawings, came a brazen warning from the Mask himself—a warning to the whole city. Then the radio stations joined the clamor. Out of loud-speakers all over the town came the Mask's ultimatum—obedience or madness!

"If you want to retain your sanity, do not interfere!" it thundered. "You, who receive orders—obey them, or take the consequences! The rest of you—mind your own business and keep out of trouble!"

"Not only that, but he is sending direct orders to my men," Kirkpatrick groaned, when Wentworth faced the haggard-eyed commissioner in his office. "Brazenly, he tells them where he is going to strike—and warns them to keep away at the specified time! I've just had a call from Lieutenant Harridge, at the Forty-seventh Street station. They found warnings pasted all over the desk and doors, instructing them to keep away from Forty-sixth Street, between Fifth and Sixth Avenues this afternoon. This is the final test, Dick. If the fellow is able to make this threat stick, the police are through—and there's more than a chance that he may succeed. The department is cracking under the strain. Suspensions and desertions are wrecking it—but there are still some of us left. As long as I can hold onto this desk, we're going to fight. The crook never was born who can wreck the New York City Police Department!"

Those words came out with a fine show of grim determination. Behind them, Wentworth could sense helpless bafflement, a desperate plea that stabbed him to the quick as he saw the poignant misery in the commissioner's drawn features.

How long Kirkpatrick could hold onto that desk was a question. Dan Daley and his committee had been on hand again that morning, demanded the commissioner's resignation and, being sent about their business by the tired old fighter, had waited on the mayor and demanded that he remove Kirkpatrick from office.

"Mayor Wallace sparred for time, but he'll have to bow to the demand if these outrages continue," Kirkpatrick admitted. "He can't stand behind me when the city is overrun with lawlessness. It isn't only Daley's committee—everyone is complaining. The bankers say they hardly dare to try to do business. The Retailers' Association claim that half their members are afraid to open their doors, after what happened at Lacy's yesterday. The Real Estate Board is protesting because real-estate values all over the city are nose-diving." He shrugged.

"This afternoon will tell the story. If the Mask gets away with this defiance, I am through. If he succeeds in staging another spectacular raid, after warning the police to stay away—"

But he wouldn't! Kirkpatrick's white-knuckled fist crashed down on his desk, as he accepted that brazen defiance. Already he was mustering his most trusted lieutenants, laying plans for thwarting this attempt to make a laughing-stock of the police department.

The Mask would not get away with it! Wentworth vowed that with equal determination, and then made plans of his own....

EARLY THAT afternoon, Richard Wentworth walked along Forty-sixth Street from Fifth Avenue to Sixth, his alert eyes inventorying every store, every building, every pedestrian, every car that passed through the block. There was no undue show of police on the street, he noticed, but scores of the department's best detectives were on hand. Strolling along the side-walk, sitting in parked cars, hidden away in stores and doorways, they scrutinized every passer-by. Ready, they waited for they knew not what to break.

Already, Wentworth had combed the buildings on both sides

of the block, studying the tenants to try and determine the objective of this latest threat. Jewelers and lapidaries were scattered all along the street, but the Allied Jewelers' Building was filled with them from top to bottom. A beehive of small offices, the building would yield a fortune if it could be looted from cellar to roof—and that, he decided, was just the sort of spectacular coup that would appeal to the Mask of Madness.

But how would the trap be sprung? How would it be—

It was mid-afternoon when Wentworth's taut nerves suddenly tingled, and he knew that the time had come!

A shrill shriek of approaching fire apparatus wailed in his ears, and he saw people running wildly along Sixth Avenue. A fire—the surest way to focus public attention and turn it away from where it was not desired.

When he reached the avenue, he quickly located the blaze in an old four-story tenement near Forty-fifth Street. Although the alarm had just sounded, the building already was a roaring furnace; smoke and flame poured from every window. All too conclusively, that spontaneous conflagration assured Wentworth its origin was incendiary. Set deliberately, it had been started simultaneously in at least a half dozen places. It had tied up traffic by cluttering the street with fire apparatus. Equipment jammed the avenue for several blocks, even down side streets.

Alert for the break he was certain would come at any moment, Wentworth walked back to Forty-sixth Street and stood beside a hook-and-ladder truck parked at the corner, just off the avenue. Except for the excitement caused by the

In a few minutes those weird-masked figures were looking everywhere.

fire, everything appeared normal. Nowhere did anything seem suspicious—until suddenly it was on top of him!

Two huge automobile transport trucks, loaded to capacity, were coming across Forty-sixth Street, carrying five cars apiece, each covered with a shrouding cloth jacket. Two trucks loaded with new automobiles—but no ordinary automobiles!

As those trucks rumbled across Sixth Avenue, Wentworth's keen ears noticed how the wooden flooring, laid on the street by the subway builders, sagged beneath their weight…. It sagged entirely too much for an ordinary load. Those cars on the trucks were not pleasure cars; they were—

No time now to puzzle it out. He had to move fast. Those trucks must be stopped! The hook-and-ladder truck—that was it! With a leap, Wentworth flung himself up into the truck's seat, stepped on the starter, throwing it into gear. But, already, the first of the big transport trucks was past, moving on toward Fifth Avenue toward the Allied Jewelers' Building.

Then he struck the second transport! Swinging the big fire truck into its path, he crashed almost broadside—sent the heavy fire truck careening over on its side.

With that crash, all attempt at camouflage vanished. Wentworth jumped clear of the tottering truck. Now he saw the sheeting, which covered those supposedly new cars, yanked away. It revealed a fleet of armored cars already spitting a barrage of death to protect the crazy-masked thugs who leaped from them, knocking loose the stays so that the cars could roll down onto the street.

The blazing guns clearing the way for them, the armored cars sped down the street, swinging into position to form a fortress in front of the Allied Jewelers' Building. Out of them now poured an army of thugs who swarmed into the building while their mates held off the police. Before reinforcements could arrive— before Kirkpatrick's men found a way to cope with this unexpected mobile fortress—the building would be looted from top to bottom. The commissioner would be through, a broken and discredited man!

But Richard Wentworth had foreseen a possibility such as this—and planned how it should be met.

DARTING THROUGH the doorway of the building next door, he grabbed an elevator from its gaping operator, jerked the control and sped up to the roof. From there, he had previously ascertained, it would be a drop of only half a story to the roof of the Jewelers' Building. The roof-house, as he feared, was locked. But a few minutes' work, with a steel jimmy, snapped the lock; and he stepped inside, onto the top-floor landing.

Cautiously, he opened the door from the stairwell to the hall. The carrier was silent, where he had expected to find it filled with terrified jewelry merchants. And then he understood why. Alongside the elevator stood a mask-faced thug, his two automatics covering the length of the hallway while his partners sped from office to office gathering their loot.

Before that sinister sentinel could whirl to meet Wentworth's unexpected attack from the stairs, the muzzle of an automatic crashed down on his head, sheared through the hideous mask— splintered the skull. Instantly, Wentworth was over the body, dragging it out of the way. Then he crouched, waiting for the others to show themselves.

Now came two more—one carrying a large canvas sack bulged with loot, the other, wary-eyed, half-crouched over the automatics gripped at his sides. Together, they stepped out of one office, started for another—and never reached it.

Too late the gun-toter glimpsed that nemesis waiting where their own mask-faced guard should have been standing. His guns roared in the echoing corridor. But even as his fingers contracted on the triggers, Wentworth's leaden slugs tore into his brain. Before the dead man had hit the floor, Wentworth was leaping down the corridor, automatics ready to blast the life out of the other thug.

But all thought of resistance had fled from that terrified looter. The bag dropped from his fingers, and he stood, whining for mercy.

"Take off that mask!" Wentworth rasped—and the moment the cowardly crook obeyed, he brought a gun down on the fellow's head.

Quickly, Wentworth stripped off the thug's dark suit, donned it in place of his own immaculate tweed. The maniacal mask came down over his head, the canvas sack was snatched from the floor, and he ran to the stairway. Racing down two flights, he mingled with half a dozen looters getting into an elevator.

Their work completed, the masked raiders now scrambled back into the armored cars. With them went Richard Wentworth, taking his place as one of their number as the bandit fleet roared off toward Fifth Avenue.

CHAPTER 10
DEATH VAULT

PEERING FROM one of the eyeholes in the side of the car, Wentworth saw that the fleet was dividing at the corner—some going north, others continuing east. Again, at the next corner, they split up, until the rest had all disappeared, and his car went racing along alone. Now there were queer noises—a sliding and clanking, banging and clicking—apparently from something happening on the outside of the car. The limited vision, afforded by the peephole, gave him no opportunity to determine its nature.

Back and forth, across town, uptown and down, they cruised, until all possible pursuit must have been eluded. Finally, Wentworth noticed that they were slowing down, swinging in and up a ramp. For an instant, he glimpsed the front of a garage—then they rolled into a brick-walled room lined with trucks.

Straight through the rear wall, they seemed to proceed—until he saw that it had raised, like a curtain opening into a smaller, empty chamber behind it. Now the masked thugs were unlocking the car's rear door, climbing out. Wentworth joined them and saw that the entire floor of the rear room was an elevator, lowering the car to basement level.

More than that, now he noticed the car's exterior. It had been completely changed, in transit, so that any attempt to identify it as one of the hold-up fleet must fail. Every step of that daring robbery had been carefully planned, completely covered, with no chance of a slip-up....

So far, Wentworth congratulated himself, his disguise had gone unchallenged. But that could not last. Already, the thugs were removing their masks; to delay too long, in following their example, would arouse suspicion.

Quickly, he glanced around the cavern. This large cellar evidently was the unloading place, for the thugs were beginning to haul the canvas sacks out of the car, piling them on the cement floor. At the rear was a door. It opened momentarily, and he heard what sounded like a woman's muffled scream from far off.

The others had clustered around the car, exclaiming over the spoils. Wentworth took advantage of their absorption to edge away toward that rear door. At first opportunity, he opened it, stepping unnoticed, into the corridor beyond. He was certain now that his ears had not tricked him. Again he caught that faint, distant scream. Somewhere, a woman writhed in agony— and, up ahead there, in all probability, was the Mask of Madness!

Wentworth's nerves were aquiver to come to grips with that murdering fiend. This was the moment for which he had been praying—the moment when the Mask and the Spider would face the showdown!

OUT OF his inside pocket came a make-up kit, and Wentworth's practiced fingers went to work, creating the marvelous transformation of which he was capable. Quickly, his features began to disappear, giving way to the hawk nose, bushy brows, lipless mouth, sallow complexion and matted hair of the Spider. Out from around his waist came the long black cape, floppy-brimmed black hat—and now the Spider was scurrying down the corridor for his prey!

Along that corridor he went, through another door, across an empty, barn-like room, then down a flight of steps to another level, his flashlight picking the way. Those blood-chilling sounds led him to a woman sobbing, another screaming in terror. They became louder, drawing him on like a magnet—until directly under his feet.

Quickly, he located a trapdoor, drew it back, and stared down at a dozen terrified people huddled together in the middle of a metal-lined wall—amongst them Catherine O'Keefe and Nita!

At the same instant, Nita spied him.

Horror leaped into her violet eyes as she sprang to her feet, raising her hands as if to push him back.

"Look out!" she screamed. "The floor—" Wentworth whirled, staring in the darkness around him. The floor… But her warning had come too late. The floor beneath him was beginning to tilt, sloping so that he lost his footing and plunged down into the doorless room below!

On his feet again instantly, the Spider started toward Nita—and was almost impaled on a shining steel rod, that suddenly shot out from one side of the metal-walled chamber, speared across the room and embedded itself in a round opening that appeared like magic in the opposite wall. It was a solid rod of shining steel, as immovable as if built into the very walls….

Even as Wentworth stooped to examine it, a terrified scream whirled him around—and another of those dagger-pointed rods silently darted out of the wall and hurtled across the room. After it came another, and another—until half a dozen of them were in place, cutting down the space in the room and separating the trembling, horrified victims.

Wentworth hardly dared take his eyes off that metal wall from which noiseless death might come lancing at any moment. Then he glimpsed the monster who operated that hellish death device. It was a madman, gaunt-faced, wild-eyed, seated behind a window set in one of the walls near the top of the chamber. Leering at them horribly, he cackled with delight as he pulled down another lever—and one of those silent death messengers streaked across the narrowing room.

"Stop that, you mad fool!" Wentworth shouted—but the grinning maniac only chuckled horribly as he bent over his fascinating toy.

Wentworth fired at the window, sending three bullets slapping against it. As he feared, the glass was bulletproof. The madman could not be stopped by that method... and those death-tipped rods were still flashing out, from one wall to the other... Some way, he must stop—

A scream of unendurable agony stood Wentworth's hair on end Even before he turned around, he knew that one of the men had been impaled—the deadly spit passing clear through the quivering body! Fearfully, the trapped victims stared at the wall from which the rods appeared, studying its surface as if to divine the spot from which the next one must appear. Now the little room had become so interlaced with bars that the prisoners were becoming wedged between them, scrambling fearfully to free themselves. The cackling idiot realized their plight and could send a steel rod within maddening inches of them—if it did not spear right through their helpless bodies.

Nita's dress was caught, Wentworth saw. Perspiration stood out on his face, as he watched her tear loose from the rod and dodge just as another glided to the very space in which she had been standing! Then one missed him by a hairbreadth, almost ripping the cloak from his shoulders, as it passed through the cloth. He tore free, climbing up on the rod, using it as a stepping-stone to another—a stairway of steel spears leading up to that little window.

He had almost reached it, when another body appeared behind the glass—a woman. Wentworth suppressed an amazed gasp, as he recognized Alicia Sprague! Ignoring the horrible sight in that torture room beyond the window, she threw her arms around the madman, pressed her lips to his loose mouth and nestled his head against her breast.

Wentworth could see that she was murmuring endearments to the fellow as she petted him. Madness faded from the wild eyes, as his hands left the row of levers, clutching her. He had forgotten his fearful pastime, irresistibly lured by the woman— but at that instant the Mask, himself, stepped into the cubby-hole!

Here was the end....

FOR A moment, the Mask towered above them in his black robe, eyes gleaming balefully from behind the hideous disguise. Then he leaped at the girl. He grabbed her by the shoulders and tried to tear her away, drag her back from the window. With a savage snarl, the madman sprang up from his seat. He flew at the interrupter, flailing with wildly swinging fists, clawing at him with taloned fingers.

The fury of that rush swept the masked man back, pushed him against the wall of the little control-room, before he could recover his balance and use his superior strength to batter the madman into submission. That was sufficient time for Alicia Sprague. Wentworth breathed deeply with relief, as he beheld her run to the window. She fumbled with the catch, then swung it open!

Wentworth covered the intervening space, gripped the casing—to pull himself through the opening and leap to the switch controlling that diabolical death-machine. Once it was disconnected, there would be no danger that the struggling men might lunge against the levers and impale the rest of the captives. Nita would escape those cruel spikes—

Nita was close behind him. Following his example, she had used the steel rods as a ladder, reaching up for the window, as he leaned out and helped her in. Then the black-robed Mask flung the madman to one side, came charging to the window, itself.

Face to face at last with the inhuman devil responsible for so much misery and tragedy, the Spider's fist flashed a blow calculated to send the hideous covering spinning from the masquerader's head—had he not lost his footing and stumbled backward, trying to dodge out of range. Frantically, he bellowed for help—and his men came running to his rescue.

There were two doors in that cubbyhole. One flung open—and the doorway was filled with lowering-faced criminals, rapacious killers wild to indulge their lust for blood. A blast of gunfire met them as the Spider's automatics blazed. But he saw at once that they were too many for him. He could not possibly stand them off, even if more of their fellows did not come swarming through that other door at his back.

That door was the only hope of escape!

Thrusting Nita behind him, he backed toward it, the room thundering deafeningly with his guns' roar.

"The door!" he shouted.

Nita had already reached it, had it open.

Beyond showed another passageway. Nita ran into it, and the Spider followed. But for a brief moment, he stood crouching in the doorway, his glittering stare a reminder to those killers what they faced if they dared pursue.

He pulled the door shut behind him, and nobody opened it. He followed Nita around a bend at the end of the long corridor. Beyond that turn a door led to stairs, and, at the top, another opened onto a garage filled with trucks and cars.

Wentworth ran to a small coupé, glanced inside and saw the keys hanging from the dashboard.

"I'll drive!" Nita slipped behind the wheel.

As she kicked the starter into life and headed for the open door, he was already busy eradicating all traces of the Spider's ugliness from his face.

The garage, he noticed, as they sped out into the street, was one belonging to the New Way Trucking Corporation—a company owned and operated by Harvey Newell!

"Harvey Newell's garage—the man Victor Hanson wants to make police commissioner of New York! Not only a weakling, but a criminal—the Mask of Madness, himself! There's no sign of pursuit," he assured her after he had scanned the street through the rear window. "It's safe now to stop at the first drugstore we pass, Nita. I want to get word to Kirk before Newell has the chance to skip."

But when his call was put through to headquarters, Stanley Kirkpatrick was not there to receive it. Incredulously, Wentworth listened to the information that came to him over the wire. Then a mighty rage welled up within him.

Kirkpatrick was no longer police commissioner! The mayor had accepted his resignation and appointed in his place—*Harvey Newell!*

CHAPTER 11
VENGEANCE OF THE
VIGILANTES!

WHEN STANLEY KIRKPATRICK walked out of the looted Allied Jewelers Building, he was a broken man. Bitterly, he had listened to the account of the latest criminal coup—realizing that the end had come. His star had set. Even before he reached headquarters, he knew what would await him there, so there was no surprise when he found Mayor Wallace sitting at his desk, staring unseeingly out of the window.

"There is nothing I'd hate to do more, Kirk," the city's chief executive said slowly, as they shook hands, "but I am accepting your resignation. I can't help myself—you know that. The wolves are howling for your scalp—and there are too many of them, in high places. The pressure they are bringing to bear for Newell is too great—" He halted now.

"Then it's Harvey Newell." Kirkpatrick's toneless words were more a dull, lifeless statement of the inevitable, than a question.

"Yes, I had to appoint him," the mayor admitted dejectedly. "He is taking charge now, reorganizing the department to cope with the conditions this crime wave has created."

Kirkpatrick knew what that "reorganization" would be, and, as he stood by and watched helplessly, his worst fears were realized. Pompous and bubbling over with self-importance, Harvey Newell was making a great show of stepping valiantly into the breach, at this time of crisis. But his orders were those of a fool, a bungling incompetent turning adrift the only men who might have been helpful.

Heartsick, now, the ex-commissioner watched the work of a lifetime being ruined, the wrecking of the organization he had built up to a model of efficiency. He realized what this portended for the helpless city. As he walked out of the big headquarters building for the last time, half a dozen of his most trusted lieutenants went with him. Then the department was left completely at the mercy of Harvey Newell—and the triumphant Mask of Madness!

BEFORE LEAVING the drugstore phone booth, where he had learned of the astounding developments at headquarters, Wentworth managed to locate Stanley Kirkpatrick at home in his apartment—where he already was planning a fight to the finish against the forces that had unseated him. Leaving the car from Newell's garage parked at a curb, Wentworth hailed a cab and gave the driver Kirkpatrick's address.

Leaning back on the cushions, he stared at Nita, trying to grasp the full significance of what had happened that afternoon. It had staggered him bodily.

"Kirk no longer the commissioner." The words came unbelievingly from his lips, as if he could not credit them. "Harvey Newell in his place. Newell, whose garage is the headquarters for the Mask of Madness—a garage rigged up with a death-room that ought to send him to the electric chair! That madman in the control-room—" he searched his memory—"there was something familiar about him. It seems, I should be able to remember—"

"You have met him, Dick," Nita said softly, her thoughts returning to that scene behind the little window. "He was Scott Crawford, a Columbia University professor we met at the Spragues," and she outlined what she had learned at the sanitarium.

"Then that probably is why Alicia was kidnaped," Wentworth began to put the pieces together; "because Crawford is in love with her and she is able to appease him, keep him in control. Just before Doctor Sprague died, he tried to say something about a madman who was loose—something about someone having carried off Alicia. It must have been Scott Crawford he meant. Probably, Crawford escaped from that convalescent home, to which he was taken—or was *not* taken there at all. If the Mask of Madness kidnaped Crawford from the sanitarium, with faked authority—and if Doctor Sprague learned of it—we have the reason for Sprague's murder that, at first, seemed to be so pointless!"

"Poor Alicia," Nita worried. "A prisoner in that terrible place, a cats-paw—"

"That was how they used her to trap Barry Winant," Wentworth's quick mind was leaping ahead. "They must have used her to trick him into an appointment there in his apartment—the appointment that resulted in his kidnaping and insanity! But who can be the inhuman devil pulling these diabolical strings? Who knows Alicia sufficiently well to figure a way to use her so adroitly for his own ends?"

These questions were still unanswered when they arrived at Kirkpatrick's apartment—then momentarily sidetracked for the ex-commissioner's more immediate troubles.

"Well, they got me, Dick," Kirkpatrick admitted dourly. "But that doesn't matter so much as the havoc they are creating in the department and the disaster coming down on the city. You don't realize the extent of the harm already done. Business is virtually at a standstill, the biggest property owners are selling out in panic, and values are toppling on every side. The city has become a place of terror. Conditions will become worse, as soon as Newell completes the sabotage he has already begun." He frowned wryly.

"I thought the man was merely a fool. Now, from what you tell me, I see that this destruction is deliberate." Kirkpatrick's eyes flashed and his jaw squared grimly. "That means he has to be stopped. We have to fight him like any other criminal—keep fighting until he's licked and exposed!"

Wentworth shared those sentiments. Now, more than ever in his eventful career of crimefighting, he realized that a tremendous responsibility confronted the Spider. With the constituted agencies of law and order crumbling, the Spider, alone, stood in the breach. He must unmask and crush this arrogant Mask of Madness—and, in that sacred duty, not fail!

There was little he could do now, in his own character—Richard Wentworth was checkmated. Those whom he suspected were all on guard against him, and he could not even get in to see the new police commissioner. Wentworth was helpless—but Blinky McQuade might still draw a hand in the desperate game. Perhaps, Blinky could again reach the Mask where even the Spider had failed....

Wentworth said nothing of his intention, as he left Kirkpatrick and his grave-faced assistants. Nor did he tell Nita the extent of his plans, when the taxi arrived at the corner of the hotel where she was registered For a long moment, they clung to each other in that embrace which was a tacit admission of the real peril hanging over them.

"I'll call you in the morning—or as soon as there is any news," he promised. Then the cab was bearing him off to the slums, to the very heart of the Mask's empire of crime.

THAT WAS a gala night in the underworld. Wentworth noticed the change the moment he alighted from the cab, and continued on foot to the murky gloom of Holian Alley. It was a night of festival and excitement—the eve of a long anticipated fete day.

Carefully, he reconnoitered Number One, but found nothing suspicious about the tenement as he let himself into Blinky McQuade's room. When Blinky emerged, to wander back to the haunts where his frowzy face was familiar, he was greeted enthusiastically.

The Bit House was jammed, China Sam's was filled to over-flowing, and, wherever he went, the hard-bitten customers were toasting the health of the new police commissioner—and laughing derisively as they downed the drink! "Tomorrow" was the watchword—but so well had the Mask established his discipline that Blinky could glean nothing more than hints of what the morrow held in store. Either those who chuckled in anticipation of its coming did not know, or they knew better than to breathe an indiscreet word....

It was almost morning when Blinky gave up the fruitless quest and went back to his room, but, in the few hours between then and his arising, a strange change came over the neighbor-hood. He sensed it the moment he shuffled down into the street. Instead of jubilation, troubled looks, the shadow of fear, was reflected from the eyes that glanced covertly into his.

"Vigilantes!" a bartender whispered as he poured a drink. "They're organizin'—a reg'lar army o' them down at city hall. Nobody knows what they're gonna do. There's talk o' them even comin' down here."

Vigilantes! Infuriated citizens were uniting to take the law into their own hands, save their city before it was swept to destruction! Was this what Kirkpatrick meant? Could this—so contrary to all his training—be his last desperate expedient to fight the triumphant Mask of Madness?

Blinky shuffled to a phone booth and tried to call Kirkpatrick's apartment, but there was no answer. Did that mean that Kirk and his friends were down there at the city hall, organizing and leading the mob?

Wentworth turned his steps westward to find out. But even before he reached city hall park, he saw that the great throng already was under way. Thousands of them, they jammed Broadway from side to side for blocks back as they headed uptown.

"Down with the crooks!" they chanted. "Down with the crooks!" That roar echoed back from the building fronts.

Despite their number, the rising mob spirit that had aroused them to fever heat, they were comparatively orderly. There was no needless violence or looting, Wentworth noticed when he detoured around several blocks and got up near the procession's head. There was no breaking into stores—until they reached the six-story arms warehouse of Landeman Brothers.

That was their destination! As one man, the front ranks halted—then were shoved on by those pressing from the rear, swept up to the doors, windows—and right through them!

Wave after wave of angry-eyed men and screaming women, they poured into the building and ransacked it from end to end—a ceaseless tide of enraged citizens sweeping in empty-handed, and emerging armed with all manner of outlandish weapons. Battle equipment from all parts of the world was stored in that building—and, when the crowd finished with it, the six floors were emptied as if by a swarm of locusts.

Rifles, muskets, cannon; swords, lances, spears, daggers, knives, war-clubs, tomahawks, battle-axes and maces—anything that could be used to give battle, that mob took with them as they resumed their march. But Wentworth was even more amazed by its leaders than by the fantastic display of the crazily assorted equipment.

This rapidly swelling army was no doing of Kirkpatrick's. Its leaders were thieves—men Wentworth had seen in the garage hideout before he made his escape—men who had been under the orders of the Mask of Madness. Now they were stirring up opposition arousing the citizens of the city, against the very regime they had put into power....

It didn't make sense...but its significance was none the less appalling. This was anarchy, the crumbling of the last vestige of law and order. The police would be helpless against warring mobs such as this. The city would be converted into a bloody battleground when they clashed with the criminal horde they were seeking.

It meant that martial law was inevitable—should be declared now. As Wentworth listened to the ominous roar of the on-sweeping mob, he wondered why the governor had not already called out the troops.

The governor! He was now the last hope for official help. Surely he did not understand the situation, or he would have intervened. He must be aroused to the danger—be made to realize what was going on in this crime-beleaguered city!

Wentworth thought of the telephone or the telegraph—but this was no matter to be taken up by wire. He must see the governor, himself—*make* him take action. And that must be done at once!

NO TIME now to go to Holian Alley. Instead, he hurried in the opposite direction, to a ramshackle building on the far West Side. It had once been a blacksmith's shop but now housed another of Wentworth's emergency cars which stood in readiness for just such times as this. Quickly, he removed the make-up from his face, took a change of clothing from the specially built compartment behind the rear-seat cushion—and, five minutes later, was pressing the speed limit in a desperate rush to the Newark airport.

The hour-and-twenty-minute flight to Albany seemed an eternity; the thirty minutes' taxi ride to the capitol building another aeon of time—but at last he climbed out at the entrance beneath the great flight of stone steps, hurried inside to the elevator and was whisked up to the executive's floor. Ushered into Governor Clinton's office, he found a broken, fear-ridden man!

"I know why you have come, Wentworth," he said miserably. "I knew as soon as your telegram arrived—but they've tied my hands. The heartless beasts have—"

Silently, he handed over a news flash that had been torn from the ticker and pasted on a sheet of paper. The dispatch reported the kidnaping of the governor's young son, Roland, from the very midst of his companions in the Albany school he attended! There was another flash—an account of the raiding and sacking of a fashionable New York finishing school. This raid had culmi-nated in the disappearance of the governor's daughter, Marcelle!

Two fiendishly calculated blows, one on top of the other—yet it was the third which had completed the governor's demoralization. On his desk lay a typewritten sheet which read—

WARNING

Both of your children are now in my hands. They are safe, unless you condemn them to the legion of lost souls by attempting to interfere with—

The brutal warning was signed with the leering soap mask of a maniacal face—a ghastly promise of what awaited his children if he did not obey!

The governor was helpless. As Wentworth looked down pityingly at the bowed head and sagging shoulders, he could not find it in his heart to criticize the broken father....

CHAPTER 12
BEHIND THE MASK

B ACK IN her hotel suite, after Wentworth had left her, Nita van Sloan paced the floor restlessly, as she wondered how she could help in this debacle that had descended upon the city and engulfed her friends. Wentworth, she knew all too well, intended to pit his wits, and stake his life, against this criminal genius who seemed so invincible. Kirkpatrick, already a ruined man, was desperately gambling all that was left in a last-ditch fight to stem the mounting tide of lawlessness.

Alicia Sprague and Catherine O'Keefe... her heart went out to the helpless prisoners of a monster to whom human life and suffering meant nothing. If only there were some way in which she could locate the two girls! But Dick had assured her that a raid on Newell's garage, even if it could be managed, would prove useless. The prisoners would be gone. No doubt even the metal-walled room would have disappeared—blown up or destroyed to prevent discovery. If only there was some way in which she could learn where those girls had been taken….

And then her prayer seemed to receive its answer!

The telephone rang. Intuition pre-prepared her for the voice that came over the wire—Alicia sobbing so that the words were hardly intelligible.

"You've got to help me, Nita!" she begged piteously. "My life and Scott's depend on it. We've gotten away from that horrible creature in the mask—but are virtual prisoners, still. If I leave Scott, they'll murder him. All I dare do is to run off for a minute like this. If only I could see you—talk to you for a few minutes—we could plan some way to rescue him. Please, Nita—"

"Of course," Nita agreed at once, "I'll help you—"

"You must come alone," the girl gasped. "Promise me you will come alone. Otherwise, we will all be killed—"

Nita promised, then jotted down the address given her. "I can be there in fifteen or twenty minutes," she assured the sobbing girl… the connection was broken.

The address was that of a house on an exclusive side street, a block or two from Fifth Avenue. A taxicab sped her to the rendezvous. An odd address, that, for someone held a prisoner. Strange, too, that Alicia had been able to get away long enough to make a phone call….

Bit by bit, she went over the girl's disjointed, half-hysterical plea, endeavoring to understand what might be behind it. It was not until she was stepping out of the taxi that she recalled that Alicia had had no way of knowing where to locate her. How could Alicia have known she was at the Raleigh, registered as Marie Cordova—

Realization came too late!

Before she could jump back into the cab, two dark figures glided across the sidewalk. They pounced upon her, carried her to a large sedan that stood at the curb, its motor throbbing. Before she had a chance to struggle or cry out, she was bundled into the car, a rough hand clamped tightly over her mouth. Then a gag was jammed between her jaws and a bandage lashed across her eyes.

With a warning shot at the taxi driver, the sedan roared off into the night....

RICHARD WENTWORTH, restlessly pacing back and forth in the Albany airport next afternoon, was able to get no response when he tried to contact Nita by telephone. She was not at her hotel, and there was no message from her. With that, he had to be content while he waited for the leaden-winged minutes to drag until the big Douglas cabin-plane would be ready to take off for New York.

He could not reach Nita, but there was somebody else who could attend to what he wanted her to do. Bob Carter, of the New York Real Estate Board, should be able to secure the information he desired. A few minutes later, he had Carter on the wire.

"I am interested in the East Twenty-second Street garage of

the New Way Trucking Corporation—over between First and Second Avenue," he explained. "Look up the ownership on that property, Bob. I want to know who owns it now, and how long they have had title."

Carter promised to get at it at once, and, as the plane winged its way back to New York, Wentworth speculated on what he would learn. What effect would the answer to that question have upon the baffling mystery of the identity of the Mask of Madness?

It was after five before the plane-connection bus drove him back to the Grand Central Station—just in time to buy the latest edition of the *Evening Standard* from a bundle dumped off the delivery truck. Even before the bundle was untied, he read the blaring headline: *Warrant Out For Kirkpatrick!* From the news account he learned that the former commissioner was now a fugitive from justice, charged with resisting the police!

That meant there was no use trying to reach Kirk at his apartment. Yet, when Wentworth called his own home, he found a message waiting there for him—supplying the address where Kirkpatrick could be located.

"Was that the only call?" he asked anxiously. "Nothing from Miss van Sloan or Ed Emmet?"

There was nothing, and Wentworth's apprehension grew. What could have become of Nita? Had the Mask trailed her to her hotel and kidnaped her in swift punishment for Wentworth's interference? Was she in the devil's hands now, or already tied up in front of that ghastly vibrator, being transformed into a hopeless idiot?

What had become of Emmet? Emmet had promised to keep in touch with the Sutton Place apartment, but now it was two days since he had been heard from....

Those questions were plaguing Wentworth as he turned into the office building at the address Kirkpatrick had indicated. A hard-eyed, elderly doorman looked him over narrowly, as he walked into the lobby. He was also aware of the searching scrutiny of the grizzled elevator operator who took him up to the tenth floor.

There was another old man at a desk, just inside the doorway of Kirkpatrick's office. A dozen more were in the big room where the ex-commissioner sat at a paper-littered desk. Wentworth recognized most of these, and understood what had been so familiar about the doorman and operator. They were ex-policemen, still indelibly stamped with the mark of the department to which they had dedicated most of their lives.

Here on the tenth floor of an office building in the heart of New York, Stanley Kirkpatrick had established an unofficial police headquarters. It was an emergency police department, composed chiefly of the pensioners from the regular department who had rallied to his aid!

"There are only a few hundred of us, so far," he said grimly, "but we already have enough to police the most vital parts of the city. The word is going around, and the old-timers are answering the way I knew they would. When this band of thieves tries to take over the city, they're going to get the surprise of their lives!"

KIRKPATRICK WAS no less concerned than Wentworth, when he learned of Nita's disappearance. Immediately, he gave the word to have the city scoured for her—but, although his veterans did their best, they were able to pick up no slightest trace of her by midnight. Exhausted with worry, Wentworth went home to Sutton Place and at last, every possible lead petered out, fell asleep with the telephone at his elbow.

There was no word that night. But, in the morning, there *was* word from the Mask himself!

Like the one that had come before, the typewritten message was glued to the outside door of the apartment that was listed in Wentworth's name but actually served only as an entrance to the building beyond. Jeeringly the mad mask of a face leered at him, when he opened the door.

This time there was no usual "Warning." Instead, he read—

CONGRATULATIONS!

Welcome back from Albany. Because you disregarded my warning, you have brought punishment down upon your own head. Because of your continued interference, Nita van Sloan will join the legion of lost souls before noon!

Before noon—and it was already nearly nine o'clock! Cold chills coursed down Wentworth's back, as he stared at that all too familiar mask. He had no doubt that this monster would keep his promise....

He must be stopped—uncovered and destroyed before he could carry out that ghastly threat! But how?

Wentworth racked his brain, and there was no answer. He was at his wit's end—helpless, at a time when Nita needed him so badly. Blindly, hardly knowing where he was going or why, he walked across town, prompted perhaps, by an impulse to see Kirkpatrick, even though he knew that there was nothing more Kirk could do.

His brain was madly churning up one desperate suggestion after the other—discarding all as wildly impossible. Then he recalled his conversation with Bob Carter. Carter should have that information, by now. In all probability, it would be worthless, but it was the only chance....

Wentworth glanced up at a signpost. Only then, did he realize that he was on Fifth Avenue, that his unconscious steps had taken him within two blocks of Carter's office... and at the same moment he realized that a gray-haired man was eying him curiously. It was a square-shouldered old fellow who carried a heavy cane.

One of Kirkpatrick's men! A block farther down the avenue, he recognized another, even though this unofficial police force wore no uniforms to distinguish them. Kirk's men had taken up their voluntary patrolling of the city's principal thoroughfares. Wentworth sensed an alert expectancy about them that whispered that something was about to break at any moment....

It might have been his own imagination, or perhaps the over-anxiety of these oldsters back in harness. He turned in at the building where the real-estate board offices were located and took the elevator to the third floor. Carter rose to meet him, as soon as he was announced. There was a look of puzzlement in the man's eyes.

"I have your information, Dick," Carter nodded. "The New Way Trucking garage doesn't belong to the corporation or to

Harvey Newell, as you probably supposed. They only lease it. The property is owned by interests who have been attracting some attention in real estate circles in the past week because they are just about the only buyers in the city. Everyone else has been unloading in wild panic. But these people have been bidding in parcel after parcel, at a song. I've been curious about them. That's why your question struck me as a bit strange—or perhaps significant?"

"These interests—whom do they represent?" Wentworth leaned close, tense. Only for that reason did he catch the name that fell from Carter's lips—for at that moment the whole building rocked with a terrific detonation... and then hell broke loose on the avenue!

There was no more time.

WENTWORTH DASHED to the front window, and stared, aghast, at the scene below. Like a swarm of locusts, the scourings of the underworld were descending on those shops so often enviously eyed from afar. Now the coveted merchandise was to be theirs for the taking!

At a given signal, they must have come rushing from their hiding places. Now all were looting and pillaging like madmen. Traffic on the avenue was at a standstill. Terrified drivers cowered in their cars, or held open their doors to pedestrians who fled in panic from those snarling hoodlums. The shrill screams of hysterical women mingled with the crash of breaking show windows, the crackle of shots.

Death was stalking down that wide street, as the unleashed devils swung viciously on any who dared to oppose them, snatching handbags and jewelry from women, shooting down men who turned to flee in hope of saving their valuables! In and out of the stores, they paraded, looting and destroying from the sheer delight of wanton destruction! Blood-thirsty machine-gunners covered any who might have attempted to interfere. This was the day for which the underworld had been waiting, the dawn of the new era when Crime should be king and the city's wealth divided among his minions!

Wentworth's jaws were clamped tightly together. His hands stole up to his shoulder holsters, as the red flame of honest outrage blazed in his heart. But Bob Carter grabbed him by the arm and tried to hold him back.

"It's no use, Dick!" he urged. "It will be suicide, if you go down there and try to cross those devils. You will throw your life away, uselessly. This city is going to need men of your caliber—"

But in that moment Richard Wentworth's thoughts were on Nita van Sloan. The devil who had decreed this hellish thing must be using it as a smoke-screen to cover his own evil purpose. Before noon, he had threatened, Nita would be turned into a brainless idiot. That meant he was working on her now....

The leaders of that criminal horde must know their master! If Wentworth could get his hands on one of them, the devil would talk if the word had to be blown out of his mouth with bullets!

By the time he reached the street, the wave of thievery had been checked amazingly. The yellow-hearted criminal underlings had lost their bravado and were in full flight, weapons spitting back spitefully as they fled for their lives.

Wentworth gaped in astonishment, as he saw the reason for

that sudden change. Kirkpatrick's men! They *had* been waiting for this outrage to break. The old-timers had met the challenge with flaming guns, and were driving the thieves down the avenue in utter rout!

With a thrill of exultation, Wentworth started after them. Then halfway out of the entrance, he stopped, just in time to avoid falling over the body of an elderly man who lay on his face in a pool of blood. It was Zeckel, the well known photographer. Evidently, he had pursued the thieves down from his studio on the second floor and been cruelly beaten to death there in the entrance.

His body lay sprawled just beneath the showcase in which samples of his work were displayed, and the splinters of the wantonly broken glass were sprinkled over him like a shroud. Wentworth glanced at that case—and the irony of it stabbed at him. In it Zeckel had displayed a photograph of Dr. Thornton Sprague, the murdered Columbia University president, surrounded by the members of his board of trustees....

In a flash, Wentworth's camera eyes took in that photograph, registered every face in it—and then something there sent him racing down the street after the fleeing thugs.

But he was too late. By the time he reached the comer, he saw that the retreating thugs had rallied momentarily. Protected by their machine-gunners, they were falling back. From the two directions, they were converging on the Public Library. He realized that this possibility had been foreseen by the cunning Mask of Madness. Even defeat had been provided for by orders to take refuge behind the stone walls of the wide-spread building which commanded the street on all sides.

Like rats the thugs scurried up the stone steps and dived between the massive pillars. The stragglers, and those who were wounded, tried to drag themselves to safety—but were blasted down by their mates before they could be taken alive.

Grimly, Kirkpatrick's fighters crept to positions behind cars, in the protection of the library wall, crouched behind the great stone lions that look out onto the street—anywhere from which they could cover the entrance and keep the thugs bottled up until the steps could be sealed and the doors breached. But that would be a long, bitter task—a battle of hours, if not all the rest of the day.

And the Mask had promised that Nita would be doomed before noon....

BITTERLY, WENTWORTH stared at the barricaded streets, realizing that all possibility of snatching one of the thieves' leaders was gone. That slim hope was dissipated, but already his frantic brain was trying to evolve another. A shadowy memory, that only half-revealed itself, was trying to warn him of some extraordinary significance.

It was the memory of old Zeckel, the photographer, lying on the street, his broken showcase behind him... that old photograph of Dr. Sprague and his trustees....

That was it—the board of trustees! It was by order of the board of trustees that Scott Crawford had been spirited away from the sanitarium and kidnaped so that his cunning brain could devise that diabolical madness machine. One of those trustees must have maneuvered that removal—one who knew the Spragues well and whose word would not be doubted!

Again memory pounded, and Wentworth recalled that conversation with Bob Carter, remembering the man named just as the thieves' onslaught had begun…. That clicked with the photograph of the trustees! It jibed with other things Wentworth had seen but not until now actually understood!

Now, he was sure, *he knew the identity of the Mask of Madness!* But he would still have to prove it, a task that might take days. And little more than an hour remained in which it must be accomplished!

To go to this devilish masquerader and attempt to prove his criminal identity would be worse than useless. Should he be able to reach his man, Wentworth knew that he would be met with outraged denial. The fellow had to be trapped, caught red-handed—chances of doing that were fading by the minute. His own judgment had failed, his estimate of human nature gone astray. He had allowed it to trick him, make of him a catspaw….

In that dark moment of soul-searching self-recrimination, Wentworth suddenly realized that his hunch had *not* led him astray—he had found the masked devil's Achilles' heel.

Hopelessly, Wentworth had gone to a telephone booth and called his home—but those words which now came over the wire electrified him, filled him with new hope. Ed Emmet had telephoned! The lad had not failed him! Eagerly, he drank in every word of the message Jackson relayed to him. Then, before it was finished, the receiver slammed back onto its hook—Wentworth was gone on his desperate race against time!

FIFTEEN MINUTES later, a somber-clad figure moved stealthily through a clump of shrubbery in Central Park. For an instant, a black felt hat poked up slightly above the bushes and an incredibly ugly face was momentarily silhouetted while the narrow, glittering eyes reconnoitered. Then the crouching figure scurried across a path and dived into another stand of brush— nodding with satisfaction when he came to an odd flat stone that had been entirely concealed by the rank growth around it.

Quickly, the Spider's strong fingers found a purchase on the stone's edge, lifted—easily swung the slab back, like a trapdoor. For a moment, he listened cautiously, then unhesitatingly lowered himself into the black opening beneath. That entrance was floored with stone and sloped gently downward. Again his fingers gripped the slab, pulled it into place above his head. Now the Spider was in the stygian blackness that seemed his native element.

At first there was no sound, only the almost palpable stillness, as his pencil flashlight beam poked around what appeared to be a rocky corridor that widened into a small cavern. Then his ears tensed, as he caught the distant mumble of low voices, the chuckle of harsh laughter, coming mutedly from beyond.

Silently, the Spider glided forward, through a labyrinth of passageways and cavern rooms that honeycombed the rocky formation beneath the park, his ears guiding him, setting him back on the right track whenever he went astray. Those rocky chambers, he noticed, showed signs of recent occupancy. They were littered with fragments of food, empty bottles—and the mute fragments of women's clothing!

This, then, was the answer to those mysterious kidnappings in the park; the answer, also, to the disappearance, from their natural haunts, of many of the underworld's most notorious characters. Those skulking devils had been quartered down here, beneath the unsuspecting city over their heads—and had reached out marauding arms to snatch mates from innocent pleasure seekers who came too close to their fetid dens!

The Spider's blood boiled as he pictured the hellish scenes that must have been enacted here in these dark caverns. Then, suddenly the voices he was trailing became louder. The tricky acoustics of the underground structure almost caught him unaware, as he stepped around a turn in the winding passage-way. He found himself full in the entrance of the largest of the caves he had encountered.

Unlike the others, this was lighted by lanterns—and popu-lated by the denizens of hell, itself!

Clustered in a ring in the center were two dozen or more of the most vicious, depraved-looking human beings he had ever seen—evil-eyed, rat-faced creatures whose natural habitat might well have been the underground burrows. An avid-eyed ring of hell's demons gathered around their high priest—the black-robed, maniacal-masked devil a terrified city had dubbed the Mask of Madness!

"I have seen you on watch up there for the past two days," the resonant voice boomed from beneath the mask, as he towered over a helpless captive who lay bound on the floor. "Yes, I knew you were there—and I knew who sent you to spy on me. That's why I let you stay there. That's why we let you see us coming in this morning—hoping you would bring Richard Wentworth down here to us. But you failed—even as human bait—and now we're through with you. Now you're going to learn what it means to try to trick me and turn your companions over to the police!"

As he spoke, his arm went over his shoulder, and a fearsome-looking blacksnake whip lashed through the air—to thud down sickeningly on human flesh, as the watching circle crowed with delight!

THE SPIDER could not see that bound captive or make out his tortured face, but he felt the blow as if it was cutting into his own flesh as Ed Emmet screamed in agony. Again that merciless whip rose and fell, again and again—its horrible blows resounding through the cavern like pistol shots. With each raising of the fiend's arm, the Spider gripped himself—resisting the impulse to leap out at the devil. He forced himself to creep forward slowly, nearer and nearer.

And then the cavern echoed with a different report. The up-raised arm stopped in mid-swing, the whip flew from it—and, before the startled watchers could get to their feet, out from the darkness beyond the lantern rays glided a nightmare figure that deluged them with death!

"The Spider!" one terrified thug howled before he pitched forward on his face—and that completed the demoralization.

Without even attempting to draw their weapons, those who had survived the deadly fire of the twin automatics that hosed them with lead, rolled and scrambled, crawled and staggered—fled from that place of sudden retribution.

"Look out for—Daley!" Emmet gasped a warning that was almost lost in the roar of gunfire.

But the Spider did not need that caution. Out of the corner of his eye he had seen the masked leader drawing an automatic, observed him raise the weapon—then it fell from nerveless fingers as a bullet shattered his arm, and the Spider was upon him.

The maniacal mask went askew, then rolled across the stone floor, to reveal the panic-stricken face of Dan Daley as he writhed in agony, clasping his shattered arm with blood-reddened fingers.

"I'm not the Mask!" he howled in terror. "I'm not the Mask—no matter how it looks, Spider! I'm not, I tell you—"

"I know you're not, Daley." The Spider's glittering eyes fixed his like those of a snake. "You wanted to be, but you're not—and now we're going to the real Mask. Up on your feet!" The prodding automatic muzzle enforced the command "Which way—quick!"

Whimpering like a whipped child, Daley started for another entrance at the far side of the cavern. For a moment, the Spider glanced down at Ed Emmet, and saw that the lad had fainted. To leave him there would be to deliver him to sure death, if any of those murdering thugs returned. There was nothing to do but take him along. With one arm beneath the youth's shoulders, he lifted him and dragged him in Daley's wake.

Docilely, Daley led the way into another passage—one barred

by a stone door that he first rolled back, soundlessly. This passage, Wentworth saw at a glance, was not natural but built of concrete. Then he dropped flat on the floor, warned in the nick of time by an almost inaudible click behind him.

The stone door had swung shut and locked. The slight noise of its closing was drowned out immediately by a terrific burst of gunfire in that narrow passageway. That blast of flame and lead scythed through Dan Daley and cut him almost in half!

Tensely, the Spider lay on the floor, listening for the slightest sound. Utter stillness followed that ear-shattering blast. But an inner voice warned him not to linger, that the danger was not past. Quickly, he got to his feet, lifting Emmet's limp body to his shoulders. Noiselessly, he glided down the long passageway—until another door barred his way.

He lowered the youth's body to the floor and felt for a latch or grip—then was flattened against the door, itself, as a terrific explosion rocked the passageway, blasting down raining fragments of cement. That blast had taken place back there in the caves and must have completely demolished them, Wentworth considered. His lips were grim as he realized how carefully the Mask had covered himself. How devilishly he must have planned to destroy those incriminating caves, and all their occupants, whenever ready to dispense with them!

Fingering the length of that metal door, Wentworth felt a slight draft near the floor. His fingertips found a crevice, worked their way in, slowly pushed the door back.

This time, as he had expected, the doorway led into a cellar, with a dim light above the down-going stairway at its farther end. Quickly, he carried Emmet's body through the doorway and stretched him out on the floor against the wall. Then he glided noiselessly across the cellar, tiptoed down that flight of stone steps, stopped at its foot—peering into the devil's own sanctum!

Seated on a bench against one wall of that subterranean room were four giggling, dull-eyed victims of the madness—Alicia Sprague, Catherine O'Keefe, Scott Crawford, his own Nita!

The four helpless victims stared with lackluster eyes at a row of those hell-spawned boxes placed in front of them—infernal madness machines operating under the watchful eye of a black-robed, maniacal-masked individual identical with the one who had been presiding in that subterranean cavern beneath the park.

"You have been useful to me, Crawford," the masked fiend was saying conversationally, "but now our little game is finished. I'm going to be sure that you do not return to sanity. You charming young ladies—it seems a shame that I could not turn you over to the men under the park. But you are too inquisitive, all of you. You have intruded into my affairs and learned sufficient, perhaps, to become embarrassing to me. It is wiser and safer to seal your mouths—and brains—for all time. When I turn you loose, nobody will believe a word you say. Nobody, for a moment will believe—"

"That Aaron Fairchild is the monster men called the Mask of Madness!" a grating voice flung at him from the doorway.

FOR AN instant, the masked face was motionless, the voice chopped off in mid-sentence. Then the black-robed body flung to one side. But it was not before the Spider had covered the intervening distance in a scrambling leap that swept those boxes off the table and to the floor. His long arms tightened around the fellow's body, as they pitched to the floor.

Savagely, the Mask fought to break free; his eyes gleamed from behind the mask; foul curses spewed from his lips—but the Spider only laughed at his futile struggles and clamped strong fingers around the devil's throat.

"Nobody would believe that Aaron Fairchild, one of the city's elite, could be such a criminal monster," he gritted. "Nobody would believe that Fairchild, the trustee of Columbia University and respected member of New York's most exclusive circles, could have schemed to set himself up as the economic master of the metropolis by getting a strangle hold on its real estate and principal industries. Nobody would believe the fantastic tale of how you used a poor, demented scientist to concoct your devilish scheme; how you used a power hungry but stupid politician to organize the underworld for you; how you brought a reign of terror down upon New York, so that its real estate values would crumble—and enable you to pick up the pieces through your dummy concerns. Nobody would believe that, Fairchild. No jury would believe it sufficiently to convict you. But nobody will need believe it now because—"

The mask had fallen from Fairchild's head, rolled aside to expose his thin, patrician features, now empurpling as his eyes popped out of his head and the tongue lolled from between slack teeth. Gurgling sounds came from his throat—that may have been intended for words but were drowned in the death-rattle.

Not until then did Wentworth relinquish his strangle hold.

Briefly, he stared down at the dead face. Then the bottom of his cigarette-lighter pressed against the pallid forehead and stamped it with the crimson symbol of the Spider. Carefully, he replaced the mask on Fairchild's head—a warning, to any who might think to emulate him, that the Spider could strike beneath any disguise! No matter how cleverly concealed, that crime would be uncovered—and ruthlessly punished—in the end!

Rising from beside the dead body, Wentworth bent anxiously over Nita and saw that her eyes were closed. Half out of the spell cast by that devilish machine, she had fallen asleep, totally exhausted by her frightful experience. But her heart was beating normally. What she needed was rest more than anything else.

The others, he saw at a glance, were much in the same condition. For a moment, he hesitated. Then he left them there, hurried up to the street floor of Aaron Fairchild's Fifth Avenue home and called Dr. Griggs, a trusted physician who could do for Nita and the others what the Spider could not.

That call completed, Wentworth rang the City Hall and waited until the anxious voice of Mayor Wallace answered him. "**I WANT** to make a trade," the Spider rasped over the wire. "The Mask of Madness in exchange for restoring Stanley Kirkpatrick to his job. Will you accept my terms?"

"The Mask of Madness!" the mayor gasped. "Kirkpatrick! You say you have—"

"Kirkpatrick has the Mask's men bottled up for you in the public library," Wentworth explained patiently, "and I have the Mask himself. He is yours, if Kirkpatrick is reinstated."

"That's all I need!" Wallace fairly shouted. "If you have the

Mask, my hands are untied. I'll have Stanley back here at his desk the minute I can lay hands on him. Who are you? Where—"

The Spider's ugly face was twisted into a caricature of a smile as he told the astounded mayor to come to the house of Aaron Fairchild for his man. Wallace was spluttering and stammering in amazement. Already, he knew, the mayor's most trusted police assistants would be on their way to investigate that seeming wild claim.

"Wait a minute!" Wallace shouted. "I don't understand! There are some other things—"

But Wentworth knew that there was no more time to lose. Before those police cars arrived, he must be gone… fading into the oblivion that was his only safe refuge.

"When Kirkpatrick goes back to his desk," he chuckled discordantly, "do this for me—give him the congratulations of the Spider!"